SPARK
AND THE
GRAND SLEUTH

SPARK
AND THE
GRAND SLEUTH

ROBERT REPINO

QUIRK BOOKS

PHILADELPHIA

Also by Robert Repino
Spark and the League of Ursus

Library of Congress Cataloging in Publication Data
Repino, Robert, author.
Spark and the grand sleuth / Robert Repino.
Summary: "A teddy bear named Spark, together with a league of toy allies, must close the interdimensional portals that leave their world, and the human one, vulnerable to attack by powerful monsters"—Provided by publisher.
CYAC: Teddy bears—Fiction. I Toys—Fiction. I Monsters—Fiction. I Magic—Fiction.
LCC PZ7.1.R464 Sn 2020 I DDC [Fic]—dc23   2020052846

ISBN: 978-1-68369-221-8

Printed in the United States of America

Typeset in Sabon

Designed by Elissa Flanigan
Illustrations by James Firnhaber
Production management by John J. McGurk

Quirk Books
215 Church Street
Philadelphia, PA 19106

quirkbooks.com

10 9 8 7 6 5 4 3 2 1

For the warriors and the peacemakers,
may their goals align

ONE

Spark sat on the shelf, her usual spot, between a set of worn-out diaries and a basketball trophy. In the window, the sun crept higher into the perfect blue sky, reflecting off the movie posters that lined the wall. It was Friday. The children were at school, the parents at work. While they were gone, Spark kept watch. Teddy bears like her were meant for this. They were meant to stay on the lookout for monsters—and anything else that could harm their human companions. This afternoon was quiet, like always. So Spark thought nothing of it when Zed—the sock monkey—called to her from the windowsill.

"A delivery guy just dropped off a package," he whispered.

Only a few weeks earlier, Zed would never have left his place on the shelf. Usually, he stayed put and begged Spark to stop sneaking around. But he had become more daring lately, ever since encountering his first monster. When he was feeling particularly brave, he boasted that he was the first sock monkey to join the League of Ursus. Spark admired this newfound courage, though his efforts to keep watch sometimes went too far. Zed was always anxious, even when the danger had passed (or was never there in the first place).

"Did you hear me?" Zed asked, tugging at the little wool cap that was sewn to his head.

"I heard you," Spark said. "Delivery guys leave packages all the time."

Zed turned away from the window. "The package just *moved*."

Spark jumped from the shelf, climbed onto the desk, and joined Zed on the windowsill. Below, a plain cardboard box the size of a microwave oven sat on the front steps.

"Delivery guy knocked twice," Zed said. "No one answered, so he stuck a note to the door and left the box."

In another hour, Zed would probably find something new to worry about. A distant police siren or a squirrel scratching on the roof. Until then, Spark would have to humor him. "Don't worry about it," she said. "Mom and Dad will grab the box when they get back."

"What's inside?" Zed asked.

"Maybe it's a new toy. Maybe that's how *you* got here," Spark teased.

Zed's mouth dropped open. This possibility clearly blew his mind. Spark realized she'd better explain before he started asking questions she couldn't answer.

"Look," she said, "have you ever heard of a monster that attacked a house from a box?" She pointed to the package, looking as harmless and bland as everything else in the neighborhood. "And how big could he be? That box is so—"

The package moved.

"—small?"

The branches outside the window hung completely still. *Couldn't have been the wind*, Spark thought.

The package shook and swiveled. Zed hopped behind Spark, his tail thumping against her arm.

"Let's go downstairs," she said.

In the hallway, Spark rolled back a section of the carpet and lifted a loose floorboard to reveal a small metal blade wrapped in a leather hilt. She pulled it free, then pushed the floorboard and carpet back into place.

"You think you need that?" Zed asked, his fingers curled around his wide mouth.

"Maybe," Spark said. Zed would be afraid no matter what, so she might as well tell the truth.

The sword was called Arctos. Sir Reginald, the bear who once guarded this house, had left it to her. He taught Spark everything she knew about the League of Ursus and its sacred duty to protect children. The blacksmith who forged Arctos had engraved the word *protector* on every inch of the blade and in every language the bears could speak. To help her carry the sword, Spark had fashioned a scabbard and belt from Dad's old leather coat. But when she clasped the buckle at her midsection, her tummy bulged above and below it. *Whatever*, she thought. Bears were not meant to be stylish. She was no Rana, Amazon Princess™.

While they hurried down the steps, the box shifted again and bumped against the door. "Maybe it's a toy robot," Zed said, "and they put the batteries in too soon! That must be it."

Spark wasn't so sure. Matthew, the oldest child in the house, would turn thirteen in a few months and had long since outgrown toy robots. His sister Loretta, a year younger, had never been interested in robots, unless they were in a movie. Spark knew Loretta better than anyone. She was Spark's *dusa*, which was the word that bears used for their best friend, the child they watched over. Loretta was creative and smart and bold. But even more important, she was kind and loving.

As Spark approached the front door, she began to worry that whatever waited on the other side had come for her dusa. It wouldn't be the first time.

Spark and Zed pressed their ears against the door. A faint sound vibrated through the wood, like mice scratching in the rafters. Spark lifted the brass mail slot. Peering through the opening, she saw the box bulge as *something* tried to push its way out.

Zed fidgeted behind her. "When do Mom and Dad get home?"

With a loud *pop!*, a pointy object stuck through the top of the box. It was a blade, sharp and shiny. Moving like a shark fin, it cut the tape from one end to the other. The lid opened, and packing peanuts spilled out. By this point, Zed's courage had completely run out. He cowered behind Spark, covering his face with his hands.

Rising from the packing peanuts was a little doll, her back to the door. Blonde hair fell over her shoulders. She wore a blue and white gingham dress, much like the Dorothy costume Loretta made for Halloween one year. Her head slowly turned toward the mail slot. She had perfectly smooth cheeks, blue eyes to match her dress, and bright pink lips. There was a pocketknife in her right hand.

Spark shut the mail slot.

"What is it?" Zed asked.

The words tumbled out. "It's the creepiest doll I've ever seen . . ."

"Oh no."

"And she's got a knife."

Zed's hands dropped from his face. "What?!"

"Here, look."

When Spark lifted the mail slot again, the doll was pressed against the opening, so close that her nose almost bumped against Spark's. Both she and Zed screamed. Spark slammed the cover shut and held it in place with both paws.

"The deadbolt!" she yelled. "Get the deadbolt!"

The doorknob began to turn. Zed climbed onto Spark's shoulders, jumped up, and slid the heavy-duty lock into place.

4

"The windows!" Spark said. She pointed to the dining room, and Zed ran in, locking each one while Spark did the same in the den. She noticed the one near the corner was open a few inches. As she tried to close it, the doll's plastic hand shot inside.

"Zed, get over here!" Spark shouted.

The doll's expressionless face tapped against the glass, as if someone operated her like a puppet.

Zed hopped onto the window frame, adding his weight. Spark pulled out her sword. When she raised the blade, the doll withdrew her hand. Once the window was shut, Spark flipped the lock. Still staring at them, the doll tested the glass with a tap of her plastic hand. Then she ran off. Whoever she was, she didn't want to leave evidence of a break-in.

"Upstairs," Spark said. "Lock everything."

As soon as she spoke the words, she heard something heavier than a squirrel scrabble across the roof.

Spark and Zed separated at the top of the stairs. She checked the window locks in Mom and Dad's room while he scampered through the children's rooms. Meanwhile, the doll's footsteps clattered across the shingles.

"It's against the rules!" Zed shouted. "A doll can't just run around like that in broad daylight!"

The doll must have known this. But she didn't care.

As Spark bolted the door to the attic, the footsteps still vibrated through the walls.

Then everything fell silent.

Zed looked around. "You think she's—"

"Shhhh," Spark said. She closed her eyes and imagined the entire house. If they wanted to keep everyone safe, teddy bears needed to memorize every inch, every hiding space, every secret of their dusa's home.

"Chimney," she said.

"Chimney?" Zed asked.

Spark ran down the steps to the fireplace and flung open the glass doors. Reaching inside, she pulled on a metal handle and the trapdoor fell into place, sealing the flue.

Spark pulled her arm free. Her brown paw was blackened with soot. She would deal with it later.

Zed appeared next to her, shaking with fear. "She can't get in, can she?"

Rather than answer, Spark headed for the kitchen, where she could see the backyard through the window. The horrible doll might appear there next.

As soon as Spark set foot on the linoleum floor, Zed screamed. She wanted to shush him, but then she saw it and her heart sank.

In the same chair where Loretta ate her breakfast sat the doll, swinging her legs, holding the pocketknife like an ordinary utensil. It was impossible! There was no way in. But there she was—toying with them. This was what monsters did. They instilled fear in their victims and then fed off that fear. Despite her appearance, this monster was no different.

Spark raised her sword. She had not yet said the oath, the sacred words that bears used against monsters.

"We are Spark," she began. Then she elbowed Zed. If he wanted to join the League, he needed to know the oath.

"And Zed," he chimed in.

"We are the sworn protectors of this house," Spark continued, with Zed barely mouthing the words alongside her. "We give refuge to the innocent."

The doll slid off the chair, her shoes clapping on the floor.

Sword raised, Spark backed away as Zed's long tail curled around her ankle. "We defend the light, to the final light, in times of darkness. By the power bestowed upon me—"

"—by the League of Ursus," the doll finished for her. She had a flat, nasally voice, like a computerized phone call. Her mouth did not move, which made her speech even more unsettling. She inched closer.

"By the power bestowed upon you by the League of Ursus, you command me to be gone," the doll said.

Spark knew then that they were in big trouble.

"What do you want?" she asked. Spark didn't really want to know. She just hoped to buy enough time to figure out what to do next.

The doll slid the knife into her pocket. She pressed both hands to her cheeks and pulled. Her face broke loose, making a sound like a suction cup. Then she lowered her mask to reveal a furry face with a brown snout and a big fat nose. A teddy bear! Wearing a blonde wig and doll's clothing!

"I suppose I want you," the bear said.

To fit inside the mask, the bear's snout had been flattened against his head. Now his nose popped outward as his snout returned to its normal length.

"Who are you?" Spark asked.

The bear's blank expression would not budge. "I am a messenger. From the Grand Sleuth."

TWO

Teddy bears were not supposed to do any of this stuff.

They were not supposed to sneak around outside. And they were absolutely forbidden from attacking a house through FedEx. The League rules kept the bears safe so they could go about their business of keeping the children safe. Bears fought off monsters—they did not *impersonate* them.

So as the bear pulled away his blonde wig to reveal his stubby ears, Spark's mind filled with questions.

"My name is Mason," the bear said. "I am here to summon you." There was no emotion in his voice. He could have been reading the ingredients in a chicken pot pie.

He was unlike any bear she had ever seen. Instead of a cartoonishly round nose and jaw, like most teddies, he had a pointy snout and leathery nostrils. He was skinny, like a bear that had hibernated all winter. Thin enough to fit into a doll disguise. Whoever designed him made sure he could pass for a real bear cub. Very impressive craftsmanship.

Mason pulled a necklace from beneath his dress: a silver pendant with two carved bear paws. One held a sword, the other a lightning bolt. Only bears who spoke for the high council—the Grand

Sleuth—could carry a talisman like this.

Spark had been waiting years for the Grand Sleuth to call upon her. All bears who proved worthy hoped to one day be honored by the council. Long ago, they had bestowed upon Sir Reginald the sword that she now carried. Before going away, Sir Reginald told Spark that no one had heard from the Grand Sleuth in a long time. They had gone into hiding. And judging from this bear, they were very good at it.

"This is how you summon bears?" she asked.

"A test," Mason said. "It always comes with a test."

Spark felt embarrassed to ask. "Did we . . . pass?"

"No. I got inside."

Zed stamped his foot and said, "Hmph!"

"*How* did you get inside?" Spark asked.

"That is for you to figure out."

"But you broke every rule to do it! What if you had gotten caught?"

"What if I had been a real monster?" Mason asked. "Do you think monsters follow the rules?"

Spark wanted to change the subject. "Look, we should—"

"Answer me," Mason said.

Spark sighed. "No, monsters don't follow the rules. Okay?"

Jeez, she thought. Even Sir Reginald would have told this guy to tone it down a little.

"You're here because of Jakmal, right?" she said. "The *real* monster we defeated."

Spark figured she was being summoned by the Grand Sleuth because of her battle with Jakmal a few weeks earlier. She had been the first in many years to lead a *juro*—a team of bears—against a monster of that size. That had to count for something.

Mason dropped his wig on the floor, where it resembled some

bizarre family pet napping on the linoleum.

"You did not defeat this monster," he said.

"What are you talking about? We rescued two children!"

"You merely escaped from his lair."

Well, if it's so easy, Spark thought, *then* you *try it.*

"Regardless, the League wishes to bestow upon you a new honor," Mason said. "Though I see you already have a sword."

Spark slid the blade into its scabbard. "This belonged to the bear who trained me."

"You will get a new one," he said. "And you will give the League a full report on the transdimensional incursion."

"The what?"

Mason snorted. "When the big hole opened up and the monster jumped out."

"Right," Spark said. "Of course. Transdimension . . . al . . . incur . . ."

"Incursion. Correct."

Mason stuck his paw into his collar and pulled out a wadded paper. He handed it to her. "Follow these directions."

Spark unfolded the paper. A detailed map drawn in pencil showed her neighborhood, with a squiggly line leading from her house to a building on the other end of town. There were instructions on the other side, written in perfect cursive, like an old manuscript.

"The Grand Sleuth is *here*?" she asked.

"They go where they are needed," Mason said.

Every bear knew that the Grand Sleuth moved around, responding to monster activity. But Spark had never really contemplated their exact whereabouts. The high council must have known about the portals opening all over town. Transdimensional whatevers.

"We're not supposed to leave the house," Spark said.

"This is an exception."

"I'll go with you," Zed said reluctantly.

"You cannot," Mason said.

"Why not?"

"Are you a bear?"

"You know, monkeys can be just as—"

"Answer me!" Mason demanded.

"He's part of our juro," Spark protested.

"A monkey cannot belong to the League," Mason said. "Bears only." He picked up his wig from the floor and placed it on top of his head, making sure to flatten his ears. Then he walked right past them, across the living room carpet and toward the front door.

"Hey!" Spark called. "We still have questions for you!"

"The Grand Sleuth will answer them. If you are willing to make the journey."

Spark caught Mason by the arm. "Hang on," she said.

"The delivery truck is on its way back."

"How do you know?"

"We phoned in a report of a vandalized package. They will take me back to where I started."

Spark had to admit: this was a clever way to travel.

"I need to talk to you *now*," she said.

"Make it quick," Mason said.

"Turn around."

"Excuse me?"

"Do it."

Mason turned to the family photos on the mantelpiece.

"There," Spark said, pointing to a picture with a golden frame, second from the left. "You see that?"

In the photo, taken the year before, the family stood in the backyard at night, a fire pit blazing behind them. Mom and Dad were dressed as Gomez and Morticia from *The Addams Family*. Dad sported a pinstriped suit and chomped a cigar. His arm was around Mom, who wore a long black wig and a slinky dress. Matthew had on a khaki jumpsuit with a plastic backpack because Dad had just shown him *Ghostbusters* for the first time. He insisted on covering himself with homemade slime, which by the end of the night had left blotches on the walls and most of the furniture. Crouching in the front was Loretta, who wore her Dorothy outfit from *The Wizard of Oz*. She held a plastic sword over her shoulder and a basket full of toy grenades. She always said that Dorothy could have used some real action-hero gear on her journey.

"Silly costumes," Mason said while readjusting his wig.

"This was taken on the Fourth Annual Amazing Night of Halloween Fright," Spark said.

Mason blinked.

"On the Saturday before Halloween, the family hosts a big costume party," Spark explained. "The kids in the neighborhood come over. Dad lights the fire pit, and then they watch a movie on the projector."

Spark remembered last year's party well, having watched from the bedroom window. Zed had remained hidden behind the books on the shelf. The costumes always scared him.

"What is your point?" Mason asked.

"They almost canceled it," Spark said. "Grandpa's funeral was the week before. Matthew had to go to the hospital again. Loretta's basketball team got blown out in a tournament. Everyone was miserable."

"Your point," Mason said. "Quickly, please."

"My point is they rallied. Loretta made Matthew his costume and brought it to him at the hospital. Mom hugged Dad and told him they should have the party even though they weren't feeling great. They stuck up for each other. The way a juro is supposed to."

Mason studied the photo again. This time, he must have noticed the bags under Dad's eyes, and how Matthew favored his right leg after another surgery.

"This is what we're protecting," Spark said. "No thanks to you."

"I beg your pardon?"

"You heard me. When Jakmal attacked, we called for help and you didn't answer. Where were you?"

Mason scoffed. "I have dealt with bears like you before. You have one moment of glory, and then you act as though you can boss everyone around. I figured you would be trouble."

Spark took a step toward him. "Oh, I'm the *worst* kind of trouble."

"It's true!" Zed squeaked.

"The worst kind of trouble is out *there*," Mason said, gesturing toward the door. "There is a war going on. Your house is one among thousands. *Millions*. Instead of puffing up your chest and acting tough, you could join us."

"But it's the Grand Sleuth's fault that Jakmal attacked us! They *made* him. He was their ally, and then they cursed him to live as a monster. He has every reason to hate us."

Spark wanted to tell the entire story again, just to see how Mason would react. "Centuries ago, there was a boy with a pair of imaginary friends," she began. "Two brothers named Jak and Mal. They were valiant knights . . ."

"I know the legend, Spark."

"It's not a legend! The bears didn't trust a child with that kind of power. They figured if he could bring his imaginary friends to life, he could bring monsters to life, too. So they cursed the two brothers. Turned them into this . . . creature."

"The bears who did that are long gone," Mason said. "Their misdeeds are in the past. Do you wish to stay there? Or would you like

13

to join us in the present? This is not about you, Spark. We have more children to save."

Spark shrank at his words. Ever since the battle with Jakmal, when she learned the awful truth of what the League had done to him, she had rehearsed what she would say if she ever met a member of the Grand Sleuth. But she'd spent so much time thinking of what she would say that she never prepared for what she might *hear*, if she bothered to listen.

Mason pulled the doll head over his face. "I have a dusa as well. His name is Damon. He is very good at karate, he is still afraid of the dark, and he loves chocolate-chip cookie dough ice cream. He is the one *I* am trying to protect."

For a moment, this strange bear seemed almost normal.

"You have your orders," he said, walking away. With an alarming speed, he scrambled up the doorframe and unlocked the deadbolt. The door opened and he slipped out, closing it behind him.

Spark and Zed peered through the mail slot as Mason hopped into the box and buried himself under the packing peanuts. Just as he'd predicted, a delivery truck pulled into the driveway to retrieve the package.

As the vehicle drove away, Zed said, "Are you really going to see the Great Sleuth?"

"*Grand* Sleuth," Spark corrected. "Yes, I'm going. I have to."

"But I'll be all by myself!" Zed whined.

"I know. But this might be our only chance to get answers."

She needed information before Jakmal returned. And his return was a question of when, not if.

A car backed into the driveway, cutting short their conversation. It was Mom, which meant the kids would soon be home from school. None of the humans would ever know that an evil "doll" had chased two stuffed animals around the house while they were away.

14

Spark would have plenty of time to contemplate her next move while sitting on the shelf. "Come on," she said.

And with that, the monkey and the bear darted up the staircase.

THREE

Loretta sat at her desk and switched on her computer. As it booted up, she coiled her thick curly hair into a bun on top of her head. Spark heard Mom and Dad murmuring downstairs.

Matthew appeared in the doorway, wearing a gray hoodie. His leg brace bulged through his jeans. One of these days, his shoulders and chest would fill out. For now, he had the skinny limbs and big head of a thirteen-year-old boy. His long hair made his face seem even narrower, which Matthew tried to correct by endlessly fussing with it.

"How's it going?" he asked, flicking his chin toward the computer.

"I need some more time," Loretta said.

Matthew walked over to her desk. On the screen, an open window showed one of her editing programs. Loretta was designing the credits for the movie they had made. Well, the movie *she* made while Matthew was trapped in Jakmal's world. He barely remembered the incident now. The psychologists and psychiatrists and therapists had all convinced him that his memories of monsters and castles were hallucinations, his brain's way of protecting itself. The adults were eager to believe that, too. They wanted so badly to return to their own safe world.

Displayed on the screen was the opening shot: a campfire in a forest. Superimposed over the trees were the words DIRECTED BY in white blocky letters.

"That's a cool font," Matthew said.

"I think it's called Trajan."

Loretta scrolled through the raw footage until she reached the closing credits, which rolled up from the bottom of the screen against a black background.

"I still have to do a proofread."

Matthew winced. "Right . . ."

The final cut was due to the Young Filmmakers contest in a few days. The year before, Loretta and Matthew had taken home the Spirit Award. But this time around, they wanted to win the top prize—Best Film. They'd misspelled the word "cinematographer" in the credits of their first movie. "That's not why we lost!" Matthew said at the time. But Loretta, the perfectionist who balanced Matthew's artistry, insisted that every typo counted.

"Are you sure you don't need help?" Matthew asked.

"I'm sure. I'll be done soon."

"Cool," he said. "Sofia gets here at four."

Sofia was Matthew and Loretta's good friend. She was also the first child stolen by Jakmal. The entire town had searched for her. Then, a few days later, Matthew went missing, too. Though they were both home again, things hadn't really returned to normal. The family had to attend sessions with a therapist, who recommended that Matthew keep in touch with his friends at the children's hospital. It soon became a weekly ritual, with Matthew running a video game tournament for the patients every Saturday. (Mom didn't approve of so much screen time, but the therapist assured her it was a good thing.) Loretta had gone with him a few times, too.

For Sofia, trying to get back to normal meant playing basketball and helping Loretta and Matthew edit the movie. She knew the software better than anyone.

But that wasn't the only reason Matthew was looking forward to her visit.

"Are you wearing your new cologne?" Loretta asked, snickering.

"Shut up!" Matthew said with a laugh. He grabbed Zed from the shelf and threw him at Loretta. The monkey's limbs flailed as he collided with her shoulder and dropped to the floor. Spark almost gasped.

"What?" Loretta said. "You gotta smell good for Sofia!"

"Are you gonna behave yourself, or do I have to sedate you?" he asked.

"Put my monkey back," she said, turning to the computer.

Matthew picked up Zed and plopped him on the shelf. Though the monkey appeared expressionless, Spark noticed a stunned look in his eyes.

Matthew paused. "What do you think Sofia wants to show us?"

"I don't know. I hope we don't have to reshoot anything."

"She sounded worried," Matthew said. "She texted me this morning. Said she found something weird in the footage."

Spark could sense that Loretta wanted to know more. But Mom and Dad had told her to give Matthew space, so she waited for him to continue.

"I'll check on you later," he said abruptly.

"Sure."

Matthew went back to his room while Loretta scrolled the credits to the part that listed the cast, which consisted entirely of stuffed animals. Spark's image appeared first, and Loretta typed her own name, since she had voiced Spark's character. Next came Lulu the panda, voiced by Loretta's friend Jisha. Then Ozzie the polar bear, voiced by Darcy. Then Rana, Amazon Princess™, voiced by Claire. Noticeably missing was Sir Reginald. He wasn't in the film because the monster had trapped him in the attic for nearly a week before Spark could rescue him.

Spark raised her head slightly to look out at the neighbor's house. Ever since Matthew gave Sir Reginald to Jared, the little boy next door, Spark checked the window at least once a day, hoping to catch a glimpse of her old friend. So far, nothing.

Sir Reginald had served the family for a long time. Many years earlier, he was Dad's bear. When Dad became too old for a teddy, he left Sir Reginald in his parents' attic for years before he gave him to Matthew. Eventually, Matthew became too old for him as well. That was when Sir Reginald made it to the final light, the moment when his dusa moved on from childhood and no longer needed a teddy bear. In that instant, the old bear became nothing more than a toy again. A clump of fake fur. Though she could not know for sure, Spark assumed that Sir Reginald had passed through the final light during his time in Grandpa's attic, only to "wake up" again when he became Matthew's bear. If Jared bonded with Sir Reginald in the same way, then he might awaken once more, just as Spark did when she first met Loretta. Still, there was no guarantee this would happen.

So many possibilities, Spark thought. And none of them took her back to the way things were. She turned back to the computer just as Loretta was entering a phrase into a search engine. A series of articles appeared about the kidnappings, as the grown-ups called them. (They didn't have a phrase for "transdimensional incursions.") Loretta scrolled through headlines like SEARCH FOR MISSING CHILD ENTERS FOURTH DAY and CANDLELIGHT VIGIL FOR MISSING GIRL.

At the bottom of the page was the headline TWO CHILDREN FREED FROM DUNGEON, KIDNAPPER STILL AT LARGE. She clicked it and an image loaded.

Loretta tiptoed from her chair, shut the door, and returned to her desk. By the time she sat down, the screen was displaying a photo of the house where Matthew and Sofia had been held prisoner by Jakmal. Loretta moved the cursor along the page and highlighted the address. She took a pen and wrote it in her notebook.

Oh no, what are you up to? Spark wondered, though deep down she knew. Loretta was conducting her own investigation. She sat for a few minutes, thinking, her fingertips massaging her temples. Finally, Loretta closed the browser and got back to work on the film credits. But Spark could sense her dusa's mind going somewhere else—to that sad, rundown house that had caused so much misery for her family. The house that maybe, just maybe, held answers to their many questions. She could not resist. She would have to find out for herself.

Spark realized that all of this was inevitable. Loretta needed to find answers, just like Spark needed to find the Grand Sleuth. Nothing was going to stop them.

Bears often took after their dusas. This time, it was the other way around.

FOUR

At exactly four in the afternoon, the doorbell rang. Matthew's footsteps pounded through the hallway. As Loretta predicted, the scent of new (but cheap) cologne trailed behind him as he passed her bedroom. Spark could imagine him at a department store getting advice from a salesperson as he sprayed it on his wrists.

Mom and Dad greeted Sofia like a long-lost relative. Even from upstairs, Spark could sense that Mom's hug lasted a few seconds too long. Like Matthew, Sofia had probably received more awkward hugs and kisses in the past few weeks than she could remember. The adults needed more time to process what had happened than the children did.

Once he pried her away from Mom's grasp, Matthew led Sofia upstairs. Loretta greeted them at her doorway. Spark had not seen Sofia in over a year. Now thirteen years old, the girl had sprouted at least three inches. She wore a blue windbreaker with her name and basketball number embroidered in white stitching on the chest. A white bandana pulled her shiny black hair away from her face.

"Shut the door," Sofia whispered as they entered.

Spark sensed a tension building in Loretta. Her dusa fidgeted and bit her lip. Then she nervously redid her bun.

"Do you have the file open?" Sofia asked.

"Right here," Loretta said, swiveling in her chair to face the screen.

"Here, let me drive," Sofia said, leaning over the keyboard. She dragged the mouse and rewound the film to the middle. "It was somewhere around here."

"That's all raw footage," Matthew said.

"I know," Sofia said. "Did you watch any of it?"

"Not really. It's mostly the girls goofing around."

"Hey!" Loretta said.

"What? It is!"

Sofia restarted the video at a moment when Claire was sitting on the couch holding Rana, Amazon Princess™ on her lap. Darcy was beside her, with Ozzie the polar bear resting at her feet.

"What was my line again?" Claire asked.

Loretta's voice answered off-screen: "The mountain pass is the quickest way."

"The mountain pass is the quickest way," Claire repeated, sounding a little bored.

The right side of the couch had been transformed into a snowy mountain range. A stack of pillows and a white wool blanket formed a snowcap, like the ones in those old stop-motion Christmas movies. Behind it, a piece of cardboard painted powder blue gave the illusion of a cloudless winter sky.

Watching the scene again gave Spark a warm feeling that spread from her tummy to her paws. She wished she could have shown it to Mason after he scolded her for failing his totally unfair test. Here was a group of young people creating something special from nothing. An epic movie filmed in a living room! And a group of teddy bears—along with a plastic warrior princess and a sock monkey—was a part of it.

The images blurred as Sofia skipped ahead. "Here it is," she said.

When she clicked PLAY again, Jisha stepped into the shot, holding Lulu by the paw so that the chubby little panda bounced against her leg with each step. Loretta tossed a script into the frame, and it flapped like a wounded bird before landing on the seat next to Darcy. "Watch it!" Jisha said, laughing. Darcy flipped through the script until she got to the mountain scene.

Sofia pointed to the corner of the screen. "There!"

Loretta and Matthew leaned in closer. "What is it?"

"Here, lemme go back."

She rewound the video a few seconds and replayed it.

"See it?" Sofia said.

"Zoom in," Matthew said. "Did you already try that?"

Sofia clicked on the toolbar. "I was about to. But then I got interrupted," she said.

"By what?"

Sofia stood up straight and faced him. "Look, I was using my dad's computer, but then he needed it. And then we got into a fight over something completely unrelated."

"Oh."

"Can we just focus on this?" Sofia said. It wasn't a question.

"Yeah, sure," Matthew said.

"Sure," Loretta repeated.

While Sofia zoomed in, the siblings glanced at each other. They knew that things were not going well between Sofia and her dad. A few months ago, she had moved in with him after her parents got divorced. He was way stricter than her mom was. After several fights, Sofia's dad had threatened to send her to another school or pull her from the basketball team. When she went missing, even Loretta and Matthew assumed she had run away to her mom's place, something she had already tried once before.

"Okay, now look at this," Sofia said. The image was zeroed in on the window on the far wall, above Jisha's head. The darkness outside created a void, flat and formless. In the blackness, something appeared and disappeared: a white oval that spun into view, catching a glimmer of light from the overhead lamp.

"What is that?" Loretta said.

Sofia slowed the video to click through each frame.

When the shape reached its full size, Spark's stomach dropped. It looked like an old man's face. The sunken eyes gave it away. Bone-white skin was pulled back against the forehead and cheekbones. Before dissolving into the shadow, the mouth opened, exposing a row of yellow fangs. It continued to open until the lips peeled away from the teeth and the jaw unhinged and dropped a few inches, like a snake eating something too large for its head.

When Sofia lifted her hand off the mouse, a film of sweat glistened on the plastic. Loretta placed her hand over her mouth. A vein filled on Matthew's neck.

The old man on the screen mocked them with his ghoulish smile. Then the mouth snapped shut, and he looked human again. But a slight wrinkle remained on each cheek where his jaw had split open. And then the face vanished—or it remained, hiding in shadow. Spark could not tell.

"Did the doctors make you draw pictures of the monster you saw?" Sofia asked, her voice trembling.

"Yeah," Matthew said.

"*That's* what you saw?" Loretta asked.

"No," Matthew said. "That's . . . something else."

"What we saw wasn't real, remember?" Sofia said. "That's what the doctors tell us."

"Sure," Matthew said. "And now, that's what we tell *them*."

"Okay, okay," Loretta said, pacing the room. "Let's stop

24

pretending. You both saw a monster. Like, for real. And I saw some-thing, too. Well, I *heard* it. And Matthew, you said you *felt* it."

Matthew pursed his lips. He probably didn't expect her to say that in front of Sofia.

"Tell her what you told me," Loretta said.

"Yeah, I felt it. Like, I could feel something nearby. It's like . . . someone breathing on your neck."

"I felt it, too," Sofia said. "Even before all this happened."

"You know what else?" Loretta said. "There are kids at the hos-pital who say they've seen monsters, too."

"Look, if all three of us go to our parents at the same time, if we show them this footage, then maybe we can convince them," Mat-thew said.

"They'll just say we photoshopped it," Sofia said. "Plus, my dad said they'll be doing tests on me for years if I keep going on about monsters. I mean, he's not wrong."

Loretta went to the computer and clicked on the web browser. It opened to the photo of the house where the children had been found. "No one believes us, but we know something weird is out there," she said. "Something's *still* out there. If the grown-ups won't do any-thing, I say *we* check it out. *We* figure out what really happened to you."

Sofia backed away from the desk. She wrapped her arms around herself and shivered violently. All of her trademark confidence had drained away.

"What's wrong?" Matthew said.

"Can't go back there," Sofia said. "I can't."

Matthew and Loretta approached their friend, each placing a hand on her shoulder.

"Please, don't go to that house," Sofia said.

Matthew looked at his sister. "We won't," he said.

"But you showed us this *thing*, Sofia," Loretta said. "Don't you want us—"

Matthew shot her a look that said: stop talking.

"Okay, we won't go to the house," Loretta said.

At last Sofia caught her breath. "I'm sorry I brought this up. Let's just finish editing, okay?"

"Right, good idea," Matthew said.

Loretta opened her mouth again, but then closed it when Matthew shot her another look.

"Let's go to my room," Matthew said. "My desk is bigger. We can all sit around and work together." He turned to Sofia. "Okay?"

Sofia nodded.

Though Loretta wanted badly to investigate this monster, she picked up on Matthew's cue to break the tension. This was why Spark loved her.

"Hey," Loretta said, "why is your desk bigger than mine?"

"Because I'm smarter," Matthew said.

While Sofia laughed, Loretta playfully kicked Matthew in the butt, which made Sofia laugh even harder.

After they left the room, Spark stared at the image of the old house until the screensaver kicked on and the screen went black.

FIVE

The glowing digits on the clock approached midnight. Loretta snored in her bed, exhausted after working on the movie for six hours straight. Together, Loretta, Matthew, and Sofia had edited all the scenes, some with as many as a dozen takes to choose from. As the night wore on, the children whittled their conversation down to a handful of words: *Yes. No. There. Go back. That one.* Their only break was when Sofia's dad called to ask her why it was taking so long.

After they finished, Matthew walked Sofia to the door. He asked for the third time that night if she would come back on Sunday, when the rest of the cast—Darcy, Jisha, and Claire—would watch the finished film. Sofia assured him that she would. Matthew tried to prolong the conversation with small talk, but they were both yawning so much that he knew it was time to say goodbye.

Soon after, the whole family went to bed. Spark could finally make her move.

On the shelf above her, Zed sat slumped against a stack of books. When she nudged his foot, he remained perfectly still. It was his way of protesting.

"Zed," Spark whispered. "Remember what I told you?"

"You told me you're gonna leave me here all by myself," he hissed. "I know you're mad, but I have to do this. You know what to do."

"Yeah, yeah."

They had agreed that Zed would press the red button on the smoke detector at the first sign of trouble. Not ideal, but Spark figured most monsters would run from the sound, which would also wake up Mom and Dad. Zed grudgingly accepted this task. Although he was braver than he used to be, he could not scare off a monster the way a teddy bear could.

Spark climbed down the shelf, pried open the bedroom door, and crept down the hall, making sure to avoid the creaky floorboards. Downstairs in the living room, she climbed the curtains to the windowsill. When she flipped the latch and lifted the window, a cold breeze leaked inside, making her shiver. She hung her legs over the side and looked down. Somehow, the three-foot drop seemed even scarier than plunging into Jakmal's portal. For the first time, Spark was venturing into the human world on her own. She couldn't count how many rules she was breaking by leaving the house. So much had changed in just a few weeks, and now she would do the impossible. Because she had to.

Spark dropped onto the grass and hid behind the shrubs. The night seemed alive with crickets chirping, streetlamps buzzing, and the distant hum of the highway drifting over the trees. Spark felt for a string in the dirt and yanked it, releasing a plastic bag she had buried there. Inside were two small camouflage outfits—one stout and chubby for her, the other long and lanky for Zed, if he ever needed it. Spark couldn't risk getting caught in the elements. Unlike the fur of a real bear, hers would be permanently damaged by rain. After the battle with Jakmal, she had fashioned a jacket and pants from Uncle Carlos's old army uniform and cut boots and gloves out of Dad's discarded leather jacket. For head protection, Spark used a child-sized bicycle helmet for herself and cut a tennis ball in half for Zed. She spray-painted them dark green to match the camouflage.

Dressed in her uniform, Spark unfolded the directions Mason had given her. The first step: head to the corner of the street and turn right. She stayed close to the house before darting across the lawn and onto the sidewalk, where she crept along in the shadows of parked cars. If anyone saw her from a window, hopefully they would mistake her for a raccoon or a skunk.

Spark stopped in front of Jared's house, which loomed like a dark gray monolith against the night sky. Somewhere inside, Sir Reginald rested on a bed, or sat on a shelf, or laid in a toy chest. Spark missed him. She missed him calling her "Hotshot" whenever he caught her showing off. Spark would have enjoyed seeing his expression if he spotted her out in the neighborhood, sneaking around like a stray cat.

The directions led to a traffic light, where a pickup truck idled under the red glow. When the stoplight turned green, the truck pulled away, leaving an empty expanse of asphalt lit yellow by the streetlamps. Spark hurried across, feeling exposed. On the other side, a chain link fence marked the border of the park. She looked in both directions. The fence went on for blocks. She would lose too much time going around the park. She needed to go *through* it.

The map pointed to a hole in the fence barely large enough for a teddy bear. After Spark slipped through, she brushed the grass and twigs off her pants and kept moving. In the darkness, the sand on the baseball field looked white as snow. She felt like an astronaut on another planet.

Something rustled in a row of hedges near the fence. Spark stopped to listen. Whatever made the noise also stopped. *Please be a squirrel*, she thought. *Or a rat. I'll take a rat. Anything but another monster!*

She started moving again. Though her night vision could not match that of a nocturnal hunter, she could see well enough. When she reached the end of the hedge, an animal with pointy ears appeared. It was a fox, raising her snout to smell a creature she had surely never seen before.

"Oh, come on," Spark whispered. "You don't wanna eat me. I'm all stuffing."

The fox crouched low and stalked along the fence, matching Spark's movement. Skinnier than a tube sock, she must have been very hungry. Maybe her pups were waiting for her to return with a mouse, a bird, or a rabbit.

Spark walked faster. She figured that breaking into a run across a baseball field would not end well. The fox disappeared into a shadow near the dugout. Spark scanned the area, straining to listen. When she felt safe again, she hurried toward the playground. She remembered visiting this place many years ago. It was here that she got to see Loretta conquer her fear of heights by climbing to the top of the corkscrew slide and then screaming with terror and delight all the way down.

A noise in the grass to her left. Spark froze. Suddenly, the fox came bounding across the field, tail and ears pointed straight back. Her yellow eyes bounced in the scant light like two glowing marbles.

Spark ran. The fence was too far! She would have to sprint across the black rubber padding that surrounded the swing set. Behind her, the fox's claws scraped the ground as she gave chase. At the slide, Spark scrambled up the ladder. The fox slammed into the lowest rung and began to climb, her teeth bared. Spark rolled onto the slide just as the fox snapped at her. Then she slid down the smooth metal, spinning and tumbling out the bottom of the chute. The fox stopped, unsure how to use this strange contraption. She leapt down and landed with a plop.

Spark reached the fence and began to climb. Halfway up, she peeked over her shoulder to see the fox standing on her hind legs, her paws grabbing on the chain links like a dog begging for a treat.

"Sorry, lady," Spark said.

She rolled over the top of the fence and dropped to the other side. The fox stuck her snout through the links and sniffed. Spark held out her paw. The fox smelled it and recoiled. Her instincts must have told her that she could not eat artificial fur and stuffing. She wagged her tail and trotted away.

Spark found herself in a parking lot illuminated by orange street-lights. She spun around and saw a gray concrete building with large windows. At the front, a crescent-shaped lane curved under a canopy, where a pair of glass doors slid open. Two women in white lab coats exited. A third followed, wearing blue scrubs and high-top sneakers. As the door swooshed closed, Spark noticed the words CHILDREN'S HOSPITAL on the glass. Off to the side was a separate entrance marked EMERGENCY.

She checked the map. This was it. The headquarters of the Grand Sleuth.

"Of course," she said.

SIX

Spark had been here before. When Matthew was younger, he spent many weeks in this hospital. He was born with his right arm and leg shorter and much weaker than the limbs on his left side. Every few years he needed another surgery, followed by physical therapy. One time, when the doctors discharged him, the whole family pretended to escape from the hospital, as if they were busting Matthew out of prison. Loretta brought Spark along. They celebrated by going to a late-night showing of *Clash of the Titans*, one of Dad's favorite movies as a kid. The adventure was among Spark's happiest memories.

Matthew still came to the hospital for follow-up visits. And his therapist encouraged him to spend time here with his friends in the children's ward. Lately, Loretta tagged along on these Saturday visits. That would be tomorrow. Well, today, technically.

Spark had never seen the hospital from this angle, and for the first time she noticed its strange design. Facing the parking lot was a modern wing with automatic doors, large windows, and smooth concrete walls. It was connected in the back to another building built many decades before. Made of yellowing brick, the structure looked completely abandoned, its windows as black as night.

The map led Spark to a loading dock behind the hospital, where overhead fluorescent lights made it look brighter than daytime. A janitor leaned against the wall, checking his cellphone. He didn't notice Spark as she slipped through the door into an empty cafeteria. A refrigerator hummed behind the counter. Spark heard voices coming from the kitchen, but the place seemed deserted.

Now the directions were very specific. She was to wait at the door for the night nurse to complete his rounds. Once his sneakers squeaked around the corner, she should run across the hall and through another doorway. This must happen no earlier than 1:14 and no later than 1:19. The round clock above the door showed the little hand on the one, the big hand near the three.

Right on time, Spark heard a squeaking sound at the far end of the hall, growing louder and closer. Peering through a crack in the door, she caught a glimpse of the nurse carrying his clipboard. Once his footsteps subsided, Spark crossed the hall and entered the next room. The door closed behind her, creating total darkness. A padded carpet absorbed the sound of her boots. The directions ended here.

A television screen mounted on the wall clicked on. It shone bright blue, like a window to another dimension. As Spark's eyes adjusted, she realized she was in a children's playroom. She could imagine the young patients sitting on the carpet to watch a movie on the TV. Picture books lined the bookshelves. A wooden treehouse stood beside a miniature kitchen set, with pots and pans, plastic burgers and drumsticks. Corkboards on the walls were pinned with children's artwork.

Spark looked down, her eyes landing on the largest toy chest she had ever seen. Teddy bears and other stuffed animals poked out at every angle. Like zombies coming to life, the bears slowly wiggled their limbs and turned their heads. One by one, bears of every size, species, and color rolled over the edge and dropped onto the floor.

Most had brown fur, some had black. Some had collars, some wore knitted socks or gloves or wool caps. A few emerged with primary-colored fur: royal blue, fire-engine red, lemon yellow.

Each bore the marks of years of service. Missing eyes. Torn ears. Patchy fur. Old stitching to reattach a paw. Every mark, every wound, told a story of how these bears had protected a child over the years. Like Sir Reginald, some may have passed from one dusa to the next, acquiring new skills and achieving feats of courage until the Grand Sleuth called upon them.

Behind them, a few other stuffed animals peeked out of the box. Spark noticed the droopy eyes of an elephant, the narrow slits of a cat. Like the bears, these toys could come to life if a child loved them enough. But the Grand Sleuth would never let them join the League. And for important meetings like this, they could only watch.

A white-furred bear stepped forward, wearing a Santa hat and a red scarf stitched onto his neck. As he approached, Spark noticed an embroidered message on the bottom of his foot: "My First Christmas."

"Welcome," he said. "My name is Iggy. Short for Igloo." He spoke in a voice fit for singing carols, not barking battle orders. Then again, Spark thought, fighting monsters required all types, and any bear with a pure heart could ward off evil.

Behind him, Mason emerged from the crowd of bears, his paws crossed.

"You already know Mason," Iggy said. "Our Hermes."

"Your what?" Spark asked.

"Messenger."

"Oh, like Hermes the—the Greek god. Right."

Iggy sighed. Spark realized that she must have sounded like some cub who'd just been recruited into the League yesterday.

"Is it safe for us to be out here?" she asked, glancing at the door.

She'd never seen so many of her kind at once, probably not since leaving the factory where she was made. Of course, she couldn't remember that far back—that was before Loretta had brought her to life.

"The door is locked," Iggy said. "If our lookouts hear the key turn, they will let us know. We are safe. And alone."

Spark did not feel safe.

"We must hear your full report," Iggy said. "It will be useful."

"Useful," Spark said. "You don't think this is over."

"Nothing is over until the final light. Until then, we are here. Monsters are out there. Now, please, we will listen."

"Wait," a brown bear said. "What about . . ." He whispered the rest in Iggy's ear.

"She'll come when she's ready," Iggy said. Then he gestured to Spark to begin.

The bears clustered around Spark, making her feel like the hub of a wheel. A few folded their arms and leaned on one foot, clearly skeptical that such a rube would impress them. The others—younger ones, with fewer scratches and scars—seemed more eager to listen.

"It started with a portal opening," Spark began. "No, wait. It goes back further than that."

She began by telling them about Sofia's disappearance, which scared her dusa Loretta so much that she began cuddling with Spark every night, like she did when she was younger. Then a portal opened in Loretta's bedroom, and Spark got her first glimpse of Jakmal. The monster had used a scratcher—a device that could open a portal between his world and this one. Soon after, Jakmal kidnapped Loretta's brother, and Sir Reginald went missing. By the time she got to the part about assembling her juro, Spark noticed the crowd making way for someone to join them. The approaching bear had pink fur, a white snout, and a bright-red ribbon tied around her neck. While the pink bear listened, the others slowly inched away from her, out of either fear or respect.

As nervous as she was, Spark enjoyed describing the traps they laid for Jakmal and the weapons they designed to fight him. A few of the bears huddled closer as she told them about getting stranded in Jakmal's world, a horrible place made of rock and lava.

"My dusa saved me," she said. "I don't know how. But she had the power to open a portal and bring me back home."

While the others listened in silence, the pink bear nodded solemnly.

Spark described the final battle, and how the portal was sealed again. She finished by explaining how Sir Reginald had moved on to the final light, just after saving his dusa Matthew. The bears lowered their heads.

When she was done, Spark realized that she had told her story in her ridiculous army outfit. She would have blushed if she could.

"What about the scratcher?" Mason said.

"I destroyed it."

Mason's mouth dropped open. He turned to the pink bear, who motioned for him to proceed. "You're sure?" he said.

"Pretty sure."

Mason didn't seem happy to hear this news.

"It's good that I destroyed it, right?" Spark asked. "No more transdimensional incursions!"

"Yes, of course," Mason said. "It's just . . ."

He looked again to the pink bear for permission to continue.

"Jakmal stole that scratcher from us," Mason said. "Which is fitting, since we stole it from the monsters many years ago. An incredible piece of technology. The last of its kind. We learned so much from it. A shame it could not be saved. But perhaps we are safer without it."

"Well, I for one think that Spark has done a marvelous job," Iggy said. "Don't you all agree?" He clapped his paws until the others joined, filling the room with the pitter-patter of their applause.

"Hold on," Spark said. "There's another monster out there. He showed up in a video my dusa and her friends made. It's as if he wanted them to see him."

"We know there are other monsters," Iggy said. "We are entering another age of conflict. And an age of conflict is also an age for heroes. Like you."

The bears applauded again. Before Spark could say anything else, Iggy motioned for someone in the rear to come forward. Out of the crowd stepped a tiny brown bear with a big head. He carried an object wrapped in cloth. The bear held it flat while Iggy unraveled the covering. The blade of a sword appeared underneath, shinier than Spark had ever imagined a sword could be.

With the weapon revealed, Iggy held it across his chest. Spark noted the golden hilt and the inscriptions on the blade. The word *protector* was carved into the metal in multiple languages. It was more beautiful than even Sir Reginald's sword. This one must have passed through many generations of bears. It was the kind of weapon she had dreamed of earning one day.

"Spark," Iggy began, "we bestow this sword upon you for your bravery."

As the light reflected off the golden handle, Spark recalled the lava flowing from the volcano in Jakmal's world. In an instant, she felt vulnerable. As if a portal could open and swallow her again.

Iggy continued. "May you carry this blade with you in your quest—"

"Wait," Spark said. "I don't want your sword. Not after what I've been through. I want answers."

The group of bears let out a collective gasp.

"Where *were* you?" Spark said. "We needed you! We called for help! And you were here the whole time. In this playpen."

"You do not understand what has been happening," Iggy said.

"Oh, and you *do*?"

The bears mumbled to one another. Someone whispered the word "crazy." On a better day, Spark would have given them a chance to explain. But all the anger she held inside shot out like air releasing from a balloon.

"The League created Jakmal," Spark said. "They placed a curse on those two brothers. Fused them together into a single monster. And that monster stole the scratcher from *you*, which started this whole mess in the first place!"

"We're trying to fix it," Iggy said.

"*Fix* it? You're supposed to be leading us! Instead you're just guarding your old secrets while bears like me are left on our own. Now there's another monster out there. And this one doesn't even care if it gets caught on camera!"

"That's enough," a creaky voice said. The pink bear hobbled toward her, using a cane to steady herself. Spark noticed fresh stitches on her joints, along with a line of stitches going right through the middle of her face. Despite her bright color, she was an older bear, holding herself together against the passage of time. The other bears fell silent.

"My young friend," the pink bear said, "I know you are upset. I remember having that same fire in my belly when I was a cub."

"I'm not a cub," Spark said.

"Neither am I," the pink bear said. She smiled long enough for it to become contagious. Spark softened her jaw a little.

"My name is Agnes," she said, reaching out her paw. "You have come a long way. Could you at least give me a few minutes to explain? Please?"

Agnes led Spark away from the others. They walked across the carpet toward the door. Now that she had gotten her anger out of her system, Spark felt a little better. She would listen, for a little while.

"You showed Mason what you were fighting for," Agnes said. "Your dusa is a filmmaker, yes?"

"That's right."

Agnes nodded. "I have been passed down, over many years, from one child to another," she said. "My first dusa would have been amazed at what yours has done. She never would have imagined such a world, where a little girl could conjure a story with her mind for everyone else to see."

Spark wondered how old the pink bear was.

"Now," Agnes said, "let me show you what *we're* fighting for."

SEVEN

Most of the overhead fluorescent lights were switched off for the night shift, leaving the hallways dim. Spark and Agnes weaved through the shadows until they reached a room at the end of the corridor. Inside, a child slept on a bed. A girl with short dark hair. Maybe six or seven years old. A row of crayon drawings was taped to one wall, along with maps of the world, a skull-and-crossbones flag, and a poster of a man with a big black beard and an eyepatch. It seemed this girl was really into pirates.

Agnes climbed onto the nightstand. She motioned for Spark to follow. The old bear leaned over and brushed the girl's hair away from her eyes.

"This is Molly," Agnes whispered. "My dusa."

Spark half expected the girl to awaken and say hello.

"Molly, this is Spark," Agnes said. "A very special bear. With a very special dusa of her own."

The child remained still. A machine by the bed beeped softly.

"Shouldn't we be quiet?" Spark whispered.

"The doctors gave her something to help her sleep," Agnes said. "We are safe."

Agnes stared at Molly wistfully. Spark wondered what had

brought the girl here. Many of the patients in this ward would never get better. Spark remembered Mom and Dad explaining that to Loretta and Matthew a long time ago. So she decided not to ask.

"What's she like?" Spark asked. It was considered a sign of respect within the League to let a bear brag about their dusa.

"Molly has dressed as a pirate for Halloween three years in a row. And counting."

Spark laughed.

"I suppose that sums it up," Agnes said. "She is an explorer. With a mischievous side."

"Like Loretta."

"Yes," Agnes said. "Molly looks up to her."

Startled, Spark looked at Agnes. "What did you say?"

Agnes gestured toward the drawings. The first one showed a blocky gray building with a red cross on it—the hospital—set under a sky colored thick with blue crayon. Standing beside the hospital was a pair of figures: one small and black-haired like Molly, the other taller with Loretta's curly bun. Molly had written her name and Loretta's on the paper, though she left out the second "t."

"Loretta and Molly are friends," Agnes said. "Your dusa comes here with her brother to spend time with the patients. That is how they met. As a matter of fact, my dusa has seen every single episode of their TV show."

Agnes meant the YouTube channel *Loretta and Matthew Love Movies*, or LM² for short. That was where the two siblings uploaded movie reviews along with short videos about filmmaking. Spark imagined Loretta playing the clips for Molly on her cellphone.

As she examined the other drawings, Spark noticed that while Molly's picture of Loretta featured bright colors, the others were mostly black and gray. In one picture, Molly had drawn a group of figures standing in front of the hospital. Spark realized that they

41

were bears keeping watch. Above them, the sky opened and strange shapes emerged from the clouds, drawn with scribbled black crayons. Demons with red eyes and yellow fangs—the only bright colors on the paper.

Most of the other drawings were similar. These darker pictures of monsters had begun to crowd out the rest. They showed the creatures spreading through the town, climbing over rooftops, marching through the streets.

"As you can see, they have much to talk about," Agnes said.

"Molly has seen the monsters, too," Spark said.

"She has dreams about them," Agnes said. "But no monster would dare show his face around here."

"That may be so," Spark said, "but Loretta's been snooping around. Trying to find out more."

"I know," Agnes said. "She has seen these drawings. And when she arrives in the morning, she will have more questions for Molly."

"You're sure the children are safe here?" Spark asked.

Agnes stroked her chin. "You seem worried."

"Well, I just thought that the Grand Sleuth would be . . ."

"Grander?"

Spark nodded.

"You've heard that the Grand Sleuth goes where they are needed, have you not?" Agnes asked.

"A few times."

Agnes paused. "I'm afraid this is another myth. We don't exactly move."

"But how do you . . . lead us?"

"Sleuth is just a fancy word for a group of bears. And there are many sleuths. Everywhere."

"So there's no *grand* Grand Sleuth?"

"There doesn't need to be. We are all working toward the same thing. So you see, we don't go *where* we're needed. We appear *when* we're needed. When the children summon us."

Agnes gave Spark a few seconds to imagine just how many Grand Sleuths there were and what they were all doing at that very moment.

"At a place like this, where children feel alone and scared, we find new dusas almost instantly," Agnes said. "They need us, and so here we are. All the children in this ward are long-term patients. Iggy has a friend named Leah. The yellow bear, Harry, he belongs to a girl named Natalie. Mason's dusa is named Damon."

"Yes, he likes karate and chocolate-chip cookie dough ice cream," Spark said.

"That's right," Agnes said. "It has fallen to this generation to rebuild the League. We're not much. And we're not perfect. I cannot hide that from you anymore. But we are trying to move forward."

"I'm sorry," Spark said. "I should not have gotten so angry."

"Oh no," Agnes said, her paw on Spark's shoulder. "Be angry, my friend. It helps sometimes. It keeps old folks like me on our toes."

Spark chuckled.

"It is true that we created Jakmal," Agnes said. "He has every reason to hate us. I cannot change that. I can only deal with the way things are now."

Spark had to admit that Agnes's words made sense. *What matters is what we do now*, Sir Reginald had often said.

"So tell me about this other monster you saw."

Spark described the horrible face in Loretta's movie.

Agnes repeated it back to her. "Bone-white skin, you said. And a bald head. A grin from ear to ear."

"That's right."

"That doesn't exactly narrow it down."

"I was afraid you'd say that."

Agnes pulled her cane closer, as if to protect herself. "A long time ago, before the League, there were monsters everywhere because there were portals everywhere. Portals to many worlds. The monsters could come and go as they pleased."

Spark had heard many stories about the days before the League. They all started this way.

"Some monsters could create the portals with magic," Agnes said. "Some needed machines. Scratchers. It took us a long time, but we beat them back. When we finally got our hands on a scratcher, it changed everything. We considered destroying it, but it was too useful. We used it to find portals and close them. It was a turning point."

"So what went wrong?" Spark asked.

"The same thing that always goes wrong. We celebrated our victories and got lazy while the monsters regrouped. They started finding other ways to create portals, or they reopened old ones. We could barely keep up. And then Jakmal stole our scratcher."

"He needed the scratcher to kidnap Loretta," Spark said. "He thought he could use her power somehow. To break the curse."

Agnes lowered her head. "He's desperate. And he doesn't realize or doesn't care that the scratcher is a crude device. The portals it creates are unstable. They've been wreaking havoc in this town, tearing at the veil between our world and all the others. More monsters have been pouring through them.

"Including the bald guy?" Spark said.

"I'm afraid so. And if Jakmal and these other monsters start working together, we'll be in grave danger. They could form an army against us."

Spark mouthed the word "army." It was a horrible thought.

"Are we talking manglers here?" she asked.

"Entire *legions* of manglers," Agnes replied.

Spark remembered Sir Reginald's description: leathery creatures with razor-sharp fangs, born from nightmares. She knew that monsters were typically too selfish to work together. But if they ever did, the Grand Sleuth could only hope to slow them down.

"I realize that the situation is complicated, but our mission is simple," Agnes said. "In your battle with Jakmal, you destroyed what we believe was the last scratcher. But as long as there are doorways into this world, then the children are not safe. More monsters will sniff them out. We must find the remaining portals and close them."

"I can help," Spark said.

"I know," Agnes said. "At least one portal in this town remains. We suspect it is close to your house."

"I can find it!" Spark said. "I know the area. I know how this monster thinks."

Agnes smiled. "That is the reason why I wanted you to come. Not for some stupid sword."

"I didn't finish," Spark said. "I'll help you find the portal if you agree to find another wizard bear who can help Jakmal. A hexen. If we want victory, we have to fix what the League did to him."

Agnes put her hands on her hips.

"You know I'm right," Spark added.

"Yes, I do."

Agnes turned away and climbed onto the mattress, leaving little dimples behind her. "You are a brave and clever bear," she said. "Few have seen what you have witnessed. By the time they do, it is often too late. By then they see the world through an old bear's eyes. They want to play it safe. They want to keep what they've earned. You have no idea how lucky you are—to be both learned and so full of life."

Very gently, Agnes pressed her paw onto Molly's forehead.

Immediately, the girl's eyes fluttered. She was dreaming.

"Now let me show you one more thing," Agnes said, reaching out her other paw. When Spark hesitated, the bear motioned her forward.

As soon as Spark touched the bear's paw, a flash of light blinded her. When the brightness subsided, she found herself in a different room—a child's bedroom. A dollhouse stood beside a miniature kitchen table, and stuffed animals sat in a row at the top of the bed. The room swayed. Spark heard a sloshing sound, like rain rushing out of a gutter spout.

Standing near the window, Molly held the giant wooden steering wheel of a ship. She wore a pirate's hat, old leather boots, and an overcoat with enormous cuffs on the sleeves. Beside her stood Agnes, dressed in striped pants and a bandana. She looked out the window through a telescope, like the captain's first mate.

The house swayed again. Spark stumbled over to the window, where she saw a blazing blue sky above an endless sea. Somehow, the house had become a ship, its foundation cutting through the foamy waves. It was impossible! Spark looked at Agnes and Molly for an explanation, but they were both having the time of their lives. Spark waved to them. They did not seem to notice.

"Iceberg!" Agnes shouted.

The sky suddenly fell overcast as an enormous mountain of ice drifted into view.

"Hard to starboard!" Molly yelled.

She spun the wheel so fast that the spokes became a blur. The ship pitched to the right. Caught off guard, Spark tumbled and struck her head on the wall. Another flash filled her vision. She covered her eyes against the light. The swaying stopped.

When Spark lifted her paws, she once again saw the tiled ceiling of Molly's hospital room. Her shoulders and legs felt cold. She realized that she was lying on the linoleum, having fallen from the bed.

Agnes knelt beside her. "Shhhh," the pink bear said.

"What was that?" Spark said. "What did you do?"

Agnes tilted her head, like a child who knows a secret. "I gave you a gift."

EIGHT

Spark needed a few minutes to collect her thoughts. While the room spun, the chill of the tiles kept her grounded. It was nighttime, not day. She lay on a hospital floor, not the carpet of a child's room. She was here now. Whatever happened a few seconds earlier was merely an illusion.

All of that sounded rational. And yet . . .

"I am sorry," Agnes said, stroking the space between Spark's ears. "I thought you were ready."

Spark tried to sit, but a gentle paw on her shoulder reminded her to get up slowly.

"You're a hexen," Spark said. "You used some kind of spell."

Agnes laughed. "No, dear," she said. "Any bear can do what I just did."

"I've never heard of it."

"But you did it yourself. In Jakmal's castle."

Spark had no idea what she meant.

"You called to your dusa *from the other side*," Agnes said. "And she heard you!"

"That's true," Spark said. Her mind drifted back to that surreal moment when Loretta answered her call and pulled her across the barrier between the two worlds.

"If the connection is strong enough, any bear can enter their dusa's mind," Agnes said. "It's not so extraordinary if you think about it. Children bring us to life. Of course we are connected to them."

"Why show me this?" Spark asked.

"Because all members of the Grand Sleuth have this power. It is a requirement. And I think you would make a fine addition to the high council one day, if you so choose."

It took a few seconds for Agnes's words to register. Spark had given up on becoming part of the Grand Sleuth. Her refusal to take the sword felt like the final word on the matter. Despite all that, Agnes was offering her another chance.

But there was more. "If you can master this power, you will become one with all the Grand Sleuth and their dusas," Agnes said. "You will see through their eyes, they will see through yours."

"That's how you decide who can join?" Spark said.

"Of course. Can you think of a better way to show your loyalty to the mission?"

"I may have entered Loretta's mind once," Spark said. "But I don't know if I can do it on command."

Agnes helped her to stand. Spark wobbled a bit until her legs grew steady.

"You will do it the same way you did it the last time. Think of Loretta. Think of what you have built in this world, and all that you hold dear. It will flow naturally from there."

"Come on," Spark said. "If it were that simple, every bear would do it."

"Nothing I said was simple," Agnes replied. "It may have come easy to you. But that was after years of service. You were training for this your whole life and didn't even know it."

Spark recalled the way Agnes spoke to Molly in the dreamworld, as if they were equals, without the rules that kept them separated. If Spark hadn't earned this same privilege by now, then no one had.

"Beats a sword, doesn't it?" Agnes said.

"I suppose so."

"I know you were close to your mentor," Agnes said. "I cannot replace Sir Reginald. But I can help you on your journey. If there's anything you want to talk about, you know where to find me."

"Thank you," Spark said.

"You should be heading home now."

"No," Spark said. "I'm staying."

"But—"

"You said Loretta will visit in the morning," Spark said. "I want to be here when she talks to Molly. If she's snooping around, I need to know what she finds out."

As she spoke, Spark pictured Zed on the verge of a full-blown meltdown as he waited for her to return. He would have to tough it out. This was more important.

"What you ask is dangerous," Agnes said. "Loretta may notice that you're gone. Or she might see you here."

"You wanted my help," Spark said. "This is how I'm helping."

Agnes nodded. "Very well. If you follow me, I can fix you up with a disguise."

She followed the pink bear toward the hallway. In the doorway, Spark glanced back at Molly lying on the bed, peaceful in her dreams. In the dark, she resembled a younger version of Loretta, the way Spark often remembered her. Protecting her in those early days meant snuggling in her arms, not sneaking into hospitals and searching for monster portals. Everything was simpler then. But there was no going back.

NINE

When he learned that Spark needed a disguise, Iggy the Christmas Bear perked up like a kid who hears an ice cream truck.

"I'm the one who designed Mason's doll disguise!" he said. "Did it fool you?"

"Um, I mean, I thought it was a doll," Spark said.

"Well, there you go."

"The knife was a bit much," Spark added.

"That was Mason's idea."

Iggy clapped his paws, and two bears appeared. "We need a hat and a scarf from the dress-up chest," he said. "Go get those socks from the baby doll—we'll use them as gloves. Be quick."

While Iggy's assistants raced about the playroom, Mason spoke to Agnes in a barely concealed whisper. He punctuated each of his sentences by punching his fist into his palm. Agnes listened patiently, leaning on her cane and nodding like a grandmother hoping to soothe a cranky child.

"Over*night*!" Mason said. "We have enough things to worry about without babysitting a stranger."

"She is one of us now."

"Can she . . . ?"

"She will. We must be patient."

One of the bear assistants returned holding a child-sized red baseball cap with the letter P stitched on the front. The other offered a forest-green knit cap and a blue scarf.

"Let's go with the green hat and scarf," Iggy said. "With the gloves it'll be the perfect fall look!"

"It's springtime," Spark said.

Iggy did not seem to care. He grew especially excited when one of the bears arrived with a pair of white baby socks. While the assistant fitted the hat on Spark's head, Iggy pulled the socks over her paws. Spark felt like a model about to march on the runway.

"Can you pop your eye out?" Iggy asked.

"What?"

"It'll help with the disguise."

"I'll take my chances," Spark said.

Just then, Agnes mumbled something that Mason did not like. He stormed off. Agnes gave Spark a look that seemed like an apology. Spark nodded in response to show that she understood. Mason was a protector, like her. Which meant he had to be suspicious about strangers in order to keep everyone safe. Spark figured she would simply steer clear of him.

With her outfit complete, Spark followed Agnes into the hallway.

"Make sure you stay in character!" Iggy said.

This advice made no sense since she planned to remain still the entire time.

In Molly's room, Spark and Agnes took their places. The pink bear sat on the wooden chair beside the bed, where Molly could reach out and grab her. Spark settled into a cardboard box in a corner, filled with toys. She peeked out just enough that she could see most of the room. Even if Loretta spotted her, the disguise would keep her safe.

The bears lay still for a long time. As the sky brightened, the hospital hummed to life. Voices began to echo through the hall, while the phone rang constantly at the reception desk. Office doors opened and closed. Vehicles parked outside, their brakes squeaking.

Molly stirred awake when an orderly wearing turquoise scrubs arrived with her breakfast, which consisted of a bowl of oatmeal, orange juice, a hard-boiled egg, and a banana. At the corner of the tray, a tiny paper cup held some pills and tablets. Without hesitating, Molly emptied the cup's contents into her mouth and swallowed a gulp of orange juice. Spark was impressed. Loretta acted like she was choking whenever she had to take half an aspirin! The orderly, a man with a goatee and thick glasses, waited for her to show that she was finished. Molly proved it by sticking out her now-yellow tongue.

"Bleh!" she said, and giggled.

"Thank you, Molly," the man said with a smile.

After he left, Molly flicked on the TV. With a Saturday morning cartoon playing in the background, she opened the drawer beside her bed and pulled out a pad of paper and a box of crayons. She selected the black one and began scribbling so fast that Spark thought the paper would catch fire. As the crayon wore down to a nub, Molly peeled the wrapper away in bits that fell to the floor. On the TV, a cartoon lion sang a song about friendship before the show switched to a commercial for a sugary breakfast cereal.

Sometime later, the orderly appeared again in the doorway. "Moll, your buddy's here." Molly slid the drawing under her covers.

The man stepped aside to reveal Loretta, a backpack slung over her shoulder. Her wrinkled navy sweater and untied shoelaces suggested that she'd thrown her outfit together at the last minute. Her tired but determined eyes all but confirmed it. After staying up late working on the movie, she had forced herself out of bed to come here.

"Are you okay for a visit?" the orderly asked.

"No, I *hate* getting visitors," Molly said, but she smiled.

The orderly frowned.

"Yes! I mean yes!" Molly said.

The man turned to Loretta. "I told you, she's learning this from you!"

"It's not me!" Loretta protested. "She was a smart aleck before I got here."

The man left, and only then did Spark accept that this was really happening. Her dusa had arrived, just as Agnes predicted. It was as if Spark had stepped into another of Molly's dreams, where anything could happen.

"Do you wanna go to the playroom?" Loretta asked.

"No, I *hate* the playroom."

"No you mean yes?"

"No I mean no."

"All right. Well, I brought you something."

Loretta set her bag on the bed and pulled out a paper tube. It was a rolled-up poster, secured by a rubber band. She glanced at the wall. "Hmm. I don't know if there's room for this with all these drawings."

"There's room!" Molly said.

With some effort, Molly slid out of bed, crumpling the drawing under her blanket. She wore pajamas and a robe. Her sleeves spilled over her tiny hands.

Loretta unrolled the poster, revealing the image of a man—a giant—dressed in ancient warrior clothing, with a sword and a helmet. He stood ankle deep in the ocean, lifting a massive ship from the water as if it were a toy.

"You said you were going to give me your *Pirates of the Caribbean* poster," Molly said.

"This is better. It's *Jason and the Argonauts*. It's an old movie. Even older than my parents."

"Hey!" someone said. It was Mom, standing in the doorway.

"Hi, Mom," Loretta said.

"Hi," Molly said.

"Matthew is running one of his video game tournaments in the playroom," Mom said. "Don't you two want to join us?"

"We're gonna stay here for a bit," Loretta said. When Mom hesitated, Loretta reassured her. "For real, Mom, we're fine." She made a shooing motion.

"All right," Mom said. "Back in half an hour."

After she left, Molly cleared a space on the wall for the poster.

"Are Jason and the Argonauts pirates?" she asked.

"Well, not really," Loretta said. "But they're on a ship looking for treasure. And they fight monsters, like this giant here. And a hydra. You know what a hydra is?"

Molly shook her head.

"It's kind of like a dragon. With, like, six or seven heads. And every time you chop one off, two more grow in its place!"

"Oh!"

"And then Jason fights an army of skeletons," Loretta said. "And they move like this."

Loretta hunched over and bared her teeth. Then she marched forward, holding a pretend shield in one hand and swinging an imaginary sword over her head. Molly laughed.

"Here, let me show you," Loretta said. She pulled out her phone and looked up a video. Spark couldn't see from behind the chair, but she heard Jason and his soldiers shouting as they battled the skeletons.

"They look so weird!" Molly said.

"I know!" Loretta said. "My dad says that he had nightmares about them when he was a kid."

"So, he didn't like it?"

"No, he loved it! He loved being scared. That's the fun kind of scared."

Molly opened a drawer and took out some tape, which she used to stick the poster to the wall. Loretta helped keep it level.

"That's why you're here," Molly said. "Because you were scared. Right?"

Loretta struggled for a moment to answer. "Matthew's therapist said we should visit. She said it would be good for us to spend time here with other kids who know what it's like to be scared."

Molly frowned.

"But I *like* coming here!" Loretta said. "I like talking to you."

"I like talking to you," Molly said.

Loretta studied Molly's drawings for a moment, her hand on her chin. "Can I ask you something?"

She walked along the wall and stopped at a picture of misshapen creatures emerging from the hospital.

"The last time I was here, you said you saw a monster coming out of the old wing of the hospital," Loretta said.

"My mom says they're not real," Molly said. "She's coming later today."

Loretta nodded. "I don't think they're real either."

Spark knew that was a lie.

"When you look out the window and you see something moving around in the dark, it could be anything," Loretta said.

"Yeah," Molly said, though she didn't seem to believe it.

"How big was it?" Loretta asked. "I mean, you draw them like they're as tall as the building. Are they really that big?"

"Can we watch another video?" Molly said.

"We will! I just wanna know. I . . . I've seen some weird things, too."

"Is that what scared you and Matthew?"

Loretta nodded. In the hall, a doctor walked by, talking loudly on his cellphone about someone's X-rays.

"Hey, what are you working on over here?" Loretta asked, pointing to the paper sticking out from Molly's bedsheet. Molly ran to the bed, swiped the paper, and stuffed it under her robe.

"Can't I see it?" Loretta said.

"Show me a video first."

"I will. Lemme see it."

The little girl pulled out the crumpled paper and handed it over.

When Loretta unfolded the drawing, her face locked into a blank expression, like a mannequin. She turned away from Molly and faced the window. When she did, Spark got a good look at the picture.

"Are you okay?" Molly asked. She sounded worried. She could see that the picture had upset Loretta.

The drawing showed a black square. Spark realized that it was the window in Molly's room. In the center was a pale man, a smile cutting across his face from cheek to cheek. All of Molly's other images had been hastily drawn, but this one was detailed. A pointy nose, a high forehead, a long chin, slightly sharpened teeth, and eyes so black that the crayon left two wax clumps on the paper.

"You saw him in your window?" Loretta said.

"Yeah."

Loretta gazed outside. The old hospital wing loomed beyond, with its crumbling bricks and plywood windows.

Molly sat down on her bed. "My mom said it was a bad dream." She didn't sound convinced.

Until now, Loretta may have told herself that Molly's pictures were simply a product of her imagination. She may have believed what the therapist said: that Matthew and Sofia thought they saw monsters as a way of dealing with whatever had happened to them.

But this picture was evidence.

"You've seen him?" Molly asked.

Loretta placed the picture on the bed. Facedown. "No," she lied. "It's just a little scary, that's all. Were you scared?"

"A little."

Loretta pointed at Agnes. "Did you grab your teddy bear? That's what I do—I mean, what I *used* to do."

"Yeah," Molly said. "Hey, you were supposed to bring yours, remember? We were s'posed to play pirates together."

"Next time," Loretta said, completely unaware that Spark was sitting in the very same room. "You know, you need to be able to draw when you're making movies like we do."

Good, Spark thought. *Change the subject.*

"You do?" Molly said.

"I told you about storyboards, right? You draw out the scenes before you shoot them? This would look cool on a storyboard for a scary movie."

Molly smiled. "Really?"

"Really," Loretta said. "Now, listen. I need to tell you something."

Molly leaned in closer.

"If we don't beat Matthew at these video games, he's going to act like he's a big shot," Loretta said. Standing, she motioned for Molly to follow her.

"Fine," Molly said. "But I wanna see another video."

"Okay."

"Can I have your phone?" Molly asked, pressing her luck.

"No."

The two children left. The drawing remained on the bed. Despite it being turned over, Spark could see the image through the paper. The eyes formed two little bumps.

"You see?" Agnes whispered. "Your dusa isn't the only one with special gifts. Mine can sense the danger in her dreams."

"And the dreams are getting worse," Spark said.

"Yes," Agnes replied. "Now you know what's at stake."

TEN

"Did you know he was this close?" Spark asked, meeting Agnes at the foot of the bed.

"No," Agnes said. "But as you can see, these monsters are getting bolder."

"I need to get home," Spark said.

"Just wait a moment. We have a plan."

The sound of squeaky wheels rolling down the hallway grew louder and louder, until a laundry cart stopped right in front of the door. Spark heard whispering. And then two sets of fuzzy ears popped up from the giant canvas basket. Iggy and Mason hopped out.

"Are you all crazy?" Spark said. "There are too many people around!"

"Don't worry," Iggy said. "The kids scatter toys all over this wing. If someone finds us, we just stay still until they bring us back to the playroom."

Mason closed the door. "Will she help us?" he asked.

"We have reached an agreement," Agnes said. "The young one will help."

With that, Iggy pulled a rolled piece of paper from under his arm and handed it to Spark. "A new map for you," he said.

Spark unrolled it. A detailed pencil drawing showed the entire neighborhood, with street names written in perfect cursive. Someone with a rougher hand had circled sections of the town and shaded them in, like clouds drifting over the houses.

"We have searched the shaded areas for the last portal," Iggy said. "As you can see, they are close to the hospital."

Spark got the point: she would search the area around her house. Sneaking out was dangerous business. They needed to coordinate their efforts if they wanted to avoid being seen.

"Jakmal is clever," Iggy said. "He hid these doorways well. They could be anywhere." He held out his paw and swung it in a smooth, horizontal line. "Look for flat surfaces. But not just on the ground or in a wall. They could be above you, diagonal, all kinds of ways."

Mason held out a cellphone, one of the old-school models that flipped open. It had a white sticker on top with a phone number. "This is a burner phone," he said. "You text this number when you find the portal, and we come find you."

"Once I find the portal, then what?" Spark asked.

"We've been studying them for years," Mason said. "We know how to close them from our side."

Iggy reached into the laundry basket and pulled Spark's army uniform from under a towel. While she got dressed, he dug out the sword and offered it to her. Spark felt everyone watching. There was little point in arguing. She had earned this honor, so she might as well accept it. As she stepped forward, a weight slid off her shoulders. This felt better than staying angry, she realized. She buckled the sword belt at her waist.

"Come on," Mason said. He led her to the window. "There's your family's car. See it?"

Spark spotted the car's silvery roof in the third row of the parking lot.

"Drop from the window here, then hide behind the bushes," Mason said. "Wait for the coast to clear, then run to the first row. Once you make it there, you can work your way to the car. Hang onto the rear bumper."

"The bumper!" Spark said.

"Hey, we've all been there," Iggy said.

Spark most certainly had not. She wanted to ask if she should just wait until dark and return the way she came, but the decision had already been made. They had no time to waste. The boldness of these Grand Sleuth bears amazed her.

Agnes had something else to say. "I'm glad you said what you said. We need to have our mistakes called out sometimes. It is how we learn. How we adapt."

"I understand now," Spark said. "Thank you for trusting me."

"Thank you for trusting us."

The pink bear held out her paw. Spark gripped it. The fur crumpled in her palm, like a weathered glove. Agnes grimaced, then straightened her face again, as if to say, *Yes, this is what I am.*

"Now find that portal," Agnes said. "Everything depends on it."

Spark climbed onto the windowsill. A truck rolled through the parking lot while a few people headed for the building. As she got ready to jump, Spark steeled herself for the mission at hand. She hated that this battle was not yet over.

Very well, she thought. *I will be the one to finish it.*

And then she leapt from the window, once again launching into a wide-open world that was no place for a teddy bear.

ELEVEN

It was a noisy, bumpy ride home. Spark hung onto the bumper with a grip so tight she thought she would dent the metal. Once the car was parked and Mom and the kids went inside, Spark dropped to the ground, slunk along the side of the house, and stashed her outfit in the bushes. Then she climbed the gutter to the second floor. She could hear Loretta talking downstairs, so she squeaked the window open. The empty space on the shelf where she normally sat looked especially wide. Above it, Zed remained perfectly still. Spark climbed to her spot and sat there as if nothing had happened.

Zed was still mad that she had left him alone for so long, so he judged her with his silence.

"I'm sorry, Zed," she said. "I had to stay."

Zed would not answer.

Sometime later, Spark heard Loretta and Matthew whispering in the hallway. And right away, she knew what it was, this secret language between siblings when they talk about things they don't want their parents to hear.

"I texted Sofia about it," Loretta said.

"You what?" Matthew said. "Dude, leave her out of this."

"We can't leave her out!"

"You saw how upset she was. That video really scared her."

"I know. But she still wants to check it out."

Matthew paused. "She does?"

"Yeah. So now you're gonna check it out, too. Right?" Loretta started laughing. She knew Matthew would follow Sofia anywhere.

Matthew stomped away toward his room. "Loretta, you are such a . . ." He replaced whatever he was going to say with a growling sound: "Uuuuurgh!"

"Aw, come on!" Loretta said, following him into his room.

Spark could make out only a few of the words. At one point, Loretta said, "Let's just see! Just to be sure!"

Eventually, Dad walked down the hall, and the conversation ended.

Like most Saturdays, the family went to a restaurant for dinner. Probably to Cavanaugh's, where Dad could watch sports on the gigantic TV screens and the kids could split an ice cream sundae for dessert.

As soon as they were gone, Spark unfurled the map onto the floor.

Zed could no longer keep still. "Is that . . ."

"The entire neighborhood," Spark said. "There's still a portal out there somewhere. We have to find it."

"We . . . *have* to . . ."

"Unless you want Jakmal finding his way back here. Or something worse."

The monkey covered his eyes and whimpered. After a few seconds, he straightened again and said, "Okay." Though still afraid, he had learned to fight through the fear. What was bravery if not that?

Spark told him what she saw at the hospital. The monkey covered his face when she got to the part about the monster from Loretta's movie appearing in one of Molly's drawings.

"We can't hide from this," Spark said. "We have to do something."

"You're right," Zed said.

It was settled, then. They would start at midnight, after everyone was asleep. They would stick to the area around the house first and work their way outward. As they climbed back up the shelves, Spark couldn't resist turning to check on Jared's house again. Night was falling, and a desk lamp cast long shadows in the boy's bedroom. Spark hoped to see Sir Reginald waiting by the window. But there was no one there.

"I think he'd be proud of you," Zed said.

"I hope so."

"*I* still say you're crazy," the monkey added.

The family returned later that night. One by one, they each settled in their rooms. Loretta lay on her bed. Her cellphone created a cone of light around her face, its white screen reflecting in her eyes. She was texting someone. The phone made a little noise with each message sent. *Eee-yoop. Eee-yoop.*

"Come on, Sofia," Loretta muttered.

Spark could hear a pinging sound in Matthew's room. All three of them were texting each other. They were planning something. The texting went on for a while until Mom walked down the hall to the bathroom. Loretta pressed the phone to her chest to prevent the glow from showing under the door. Once Mom passed, Loretta scrolled to the clock and set the alarm for one in the morning. She set the phone on her pillow and dozed off. Oddly, she was still wearing her clothes, and had left her sneakers next to the bed.

A few minutes before midnight, Zed tapped Spark on her head. "Are we going?"

"New plan," Spark whispered. "I want to see what they're up to."

At one a.m., Loretta's alarm buzzed. She grabbed her phone and switched it off. Then she rolled out of bed and slipped into her shoes. Using the phone's flashlight, she opened a drawer and pulled out her Swiss army knife, the one Dad gave her. It had her initials carved into the green handle. Spark had no idea what Loretta expected to do with it, but the way she stuffed the knife into her pocket made it seem as though she was preparing for battle.

Loretta grabbed her jacket and tiptoed out the door. A few seconds later, Spark heard Matthew's footsteps in the hall.

"Where are they going?" Zed said.

Spark went to the window. At the corner, someone waited beneath the streetlamp, their face obscured by the hood of their jacket. Loretta and Matthew emerged from the shadow of their house, headed for the corner.

"That's Sofia," Spark said.

She opened the window.

"What are you doing?" Zed said.

"Going after them. They're looking for monsters. I have to make sure they don't find one."

"Should . . . should I go?" Zed's tone suggested that he desperately wanted her to say no.

"Stay here," she said. "If I'm not back by three, set off the smoke detector."

Zed nodded frantically.

Perched on the ledge, Spark readied herself. Once again, she looked at Jared's window, hoping to find Sir Reginald there. But nothing appeared. She was in charge for good.

TWELVE

For her entire life, Spark felt proud to have a dusa like Loretta, one who possessed a keen, curious mind and an adventurous spirit. But as she trailed behind the three friends, Spark found herself regretting having such an active child to look after. Bears who protected readers and video gamers had it easy.

When the children made a right on Bond and a left on Penn, Spark knew for certain where they were going. The hospital. More specifically, the abandoned wing, where Molly had seen something she could not explain. Even if it was all a dream, the figure was the same as the one Loretta had caught on camera. At best, this was a waste of time, for surely the Grand Sleuth had already checked every inch of the place. At worst, the creepy, dead-eyed monster with the white face and the wide smile would be there.

Maybe he had laid a trap for them.

Spark kept hidden by walking in the street, behind the parked cars. All the while, she tried to think of something that would scare the children into going back home. She tried to concentrate, like Agnes had taught her. If she could connect with Loretta the way Agnes did with Molly, maybe she'd get her dusa to see that this was a mistake. But they were moving fast, and Spark was struggling to keep up. She was too distracted.

When a vehicle passed, the children took cover behind a row of bushes. Like Spark, they couldn't risk getting caught. Matthew rose from his crouch just as a truck came around the corner. Loretta tugged his shirt and forced him down again.

"Yo!" he hissed.

"Be careful!" she said.

"It's gonna take all night if we have to hide every five minutes!"

"Then it'll take all night!"

Rather than join their debate, Sofia got up and walked away. The siblings stopped arguing. Matthew gave his sister a look that said, *See what you did?*

Spark wondered what had changed Sofia's mind about joining their investigation. The girl was quiet and serious, as though she just wanted to get it over with. No games, no jokes, no arguing. As they all had admitted the night before, they could sense the monsters nearby. They needed to get to the bottom of things, or the feeling would keep creeping up on them, getting worse all the time.

Every few blocks, Loretta peeked over her shoulder. Maybe she could hear Spark—or sense her somehow. After what Agnes had shown her, anything seemed possible.

"Are you remembering anything?" Loretta asked Matthew. "Does any of this look familiar?"

Spark realized that they were only a few blocks away from the house where Jakmal kept them.

"I don't remember," Matthew said.

Sofia shook her head. "We didn't come this way."

"Did he take you through the cemetery?" Loretta asked.

"He didn't take me through anything. Or over anything. Or around. One minute, I was in my room. The next minute, I was someplace else."

"Same here," Matthew said. "We've been over this already."

"So he, like, hypnotized you," Loretta said.

"I read an article that said hypnosis isn't real," Matthew said. "It's a trick."

"It's totally real. I've seen it."

"Yeah, on TV. On a reality show."

"Yeah, *reality*!"

"Quiet, you two!" Sofia hissed. "Nobody cares."

The debate ended when the children arrived at the entrance to the park. Spark wanted to warn them about the fox but then remembered that the animal would run away from humans. So she followed behind, using the darkness for cover. When the children reached the other side, they waited at the chain-link fence and surveyed the nearly empty hospital parking lot.

Matthew had taken them on a route different from Spark's. Here, they faced the spot where the new concrete hospital connected to the old brick wing. A wall made of plywood had been built around this section, like a shell. On it, a poster for a construction company announced that the wing would be rebuilt that summer. The security lights turned the children into silhouettes. From Spark's perspective, they looked as tall as grown-ups.

"When I was a patient here, me and the other kids would stay up late, after lights out," Matthew said. "We used to take bets on who was brave enough to sneak inside."

"Did you win?" Sofia asked.

"Oh, yeah. Everyone owed me a chocolate bar. They all got stuck in the vending machine, though."

"You're sure there are no cameras," Loretta said.

"They're only in the front," Matthew replied. "Should be fine here."

Please, Spark thought. *Please, just turn back. This is a bad idea.*

But was it? If anyone had the right to seek out answers, it was these three children.

The girls helped Matthew climb the fence. At the top, he swung his strong leg over first, then hung from the other side before lowering to the ground. Loretta went next, struggling a bit. Sofia, the best athlete in the group, cleared the obstacle in seconds.

One by one, they reached into their pockets and turned on the flashlights on their phones. At the plywood wall, the gaps between the panels allowed them to peek inside. Spark waited on the other side of the fence.

In the center of the plywood wall was a makeshift door sealed with a large padlock and chain. Matthew tilted the door diagonally, creating a wide gap at the bottom. Whoever built it hadn't expected children to break in.

Matthew got on his hands and knees to squeeze his way inside.

"Matthew, wait!" Loretta said.

"This was *your* idea!" he called back. "We're here, no one's around. So let's check it out!"

There was an anger in his voice that Spark had not heard in some time. He was fed up with all the adults in his life badgering him with questions he couldn't answer. That anger now overpowered his fear. He needed to know.

And if he went in, then Loretta would go, too. Sofia followed, either to watch over them or to avoid being left alone. Spark could not stop them. She could barely keep track of them. This was how it started, she realized. The children had waited their entire lives to decide things for themselves, and now they were finally doing it.

Spark scrambled over the fence and dropped to the asphalt. She approached the opening in the plywood wall cautiously, listening first. Inside, a set of metal doors hung open—this must have been the main entrance to the hospital before the reconstruction began.

Passing through the archway, Spark entered an old lobby area. Two shadowy figures appeared on either side. She retreated, shaking with dread. But they didn't follow her. When she stepped inside again, she found that the giants were merely statues, an angel on either side of the entrance. One of them had its nose broken off. The other was missing part of its wing. In the scant light from the parking lot, their faces appeared hardened and menacing, as if modeled off soldiers marching into battle. Their smooth eyes seemed to be watching her.

The three children had stopped at the ancient wooden reception desk, where they pointed their flashlights at an even creepier sculpture that hung from the back wall. There, a man held a staff with two snakes coiled around it. Spark knew that this represented a doctor, though she could not remember what the snakes had to do with medicine. The man used the staff to ward off a ghastly, skinny creature—a skeleton, its jaw hinging open. Spark assumed that the sculptor intended to make people feel safe with this image. But the skeleton did not seem as scared as he should be. In fact, he appeared ready to lunge at the man with the staff and overpower him.

"Keep the flashlights down," Loretta whispered.

"I can't explain it," Matthew said, "but there's something really bad here. It's like . . . familiar. You know what I mean?"

With growing horror, Spark realized that she knew exactly what he meant. She could smell rust and grease—the scent of monsters.

Sofia nodded a few times but could not say the word. Sensing her fear, Matthew stepped closer, offering his hand.

"We can go back," he said.

Yes! Spark thought. *Yes, go back!*

"I'm fine," Sofia said.

They inched toward a stairway to the basement, which led to a blackness that swallowed the beams from their flashlights.

Just then, Spark thought she saw something move right beside her. The angels. One of them looked different. Had it shifted? The statue seemed to lean a little closer to the children, its head tilted. Maybe its wings spread a little farther—or maybe Spark imagined it. A trick of the light, perhaps.

All right, this has gone far enough, Spark thought. Yes, she needed to let the children grow up. But maybe *after* she got them out of here. Spark fell back to the entrance, frantically looking around for anything she could use to scare them off. A rock she could throw through a window. Or a twig she could toss into the stairwell.

Instead of a twig or a stone, she spotted something that was far more likely to scare the kids: a car, slowly turning the corner of the building. A row of yellow lights sat atop the roof, and a logo on the door depicted a giant bird of prey swooping over a gold shield: Eagle Security Services.

"Oh dear," she said. This wasn't the kind of distraction she had in mind.

A walkie-talkie chittered from inside the car. *Kuk!* "10-23," a man said. "Checking the old wing."

Kuk! "10-4," the dispatcher said. "Car 109 en route."

"Copy."

The car parked and the doors opened. Two security guards in baseball caps and khaki pants stood on the threshold. One of the guards had a fat red nose and a salt-and-pepper mustache. The other looked like he was barely out of high school. A rookie, Spark guessed. Mustache pulled a long black flashlight from his belt and clicked it on. Spark, half hidden behind the plywood door, dropped in a lifeless heap just in time as the light passed over her. For a few seconds, the officer examined this strange teddy bear wearing a soldier's uniform.

"Cute," he said, before strolling into the lobby. Spark considered untying the lace on his black shoes, but the moment passed. She felt the vibrations of his footsteps through the floor.

Meanwhile, all the noise from inside had stopped. Spark could imagine the children taking one final glance at each other before flicking off their lights and awaiting their fate—whatever that was. Spark had no idea.

So she decided to stop it. Though the League had rules against interfering in human affairs unless children were in danger, none of that seemed fair. The children just wanted to learn. They didn't deserve to be punished for it.

As soon as Officer Rookie entered the building, Spark bolted for the car. She jumped and grabbed the passenger door handle, but it was locked. Of course. Rookie did the right thing. He knew he'd get in trouble for leaving it unlocked.

But not Mustache. Maybe he'd gotten lazy. Maybe he had only a few months left before retirement and just didn't follow all the rules anymore. When Spark pulled on the driver-side door handle, it opened with a satisfying pop. She planted her boots on the frame and pulled it open until she could squeeze inside.

She hopped onto the warm leather seat. Two coffee cups steamed in the cupholder, and a clipboard sat on top of the dashboard.

From watching movies, Spark possessed a general knowledge of how to drive a car. Spin the wheel to make it turn. Press the tall pedal to make it go, the wide pedal to make it stop. Fiddle with the gearshift behind the steering column to point the car forward or backward. But a teddy bear could not do all of these things at once.

She reached for what she thought was the gearshift and cranked it toward the floor. Instead of moving the car, it switched on the windshield wipers. The rubber squeegees dragged across the dry glass.

Hearing the squeaking noise, Mustache stepped out of the building. "What the . . . ?"

Spark tried again, this time with the other lever. Of course it was the longer one! Everyone knew that. She hung from the knob at the end until the lever dropped. She slid off just as the car lurched into drive.

"Hey!" Mustache shouted.

The car did not obey. It rolled away from the officer as he ran alongside it, shouting into his walkie-talkie.

"10-31, 10-31! I got a suspect hijacking my car!" *Kuk!*

It was funny how even the slightest incline could allow a vehicle to gather so much speed. After a few seconds, it felt as if Spark had floored the gas pedal. Mustache managed to open the passenger door, but by then the vehicle was moving so fast he couldn't keep up. As the man stumbled, the car veered toward the curb and hopped it, bouncing Spark so high that she hit the ceiling before landing on the seat again. When she peeked over the dashboard, she saw that the car had now veered in the other direction, headed straight for the fence. She ducked as it collided with a pole, bending the metal inward.

The door flopped open and the siren began to whirr. *Wee-ow, wee-ow, wee-ow.* The yellow lights on top of the car spun around. Spark dizzily climbed out. Footsteps approached—first the heavy shoes of Mustache, followed close behind by Rookie.

Spark rolled under the car and waited while the two officers pointed their flashlights inside. Like so many other grown-ups confronted with something they could not understand, they dismissed it as a mere accident. An oversight. A malfunction.

Meanwhile, unbeknownst to them, three small figures slipped out of the abandoned hospital and ran off into the night.

Kuk! "Car 85, come in. Car 85—"

"Ya gonna answer that?" the Rookie asked.

"No," Mustache said.

THIRTEEN

More security guards arrived at the scene. Poor Mustache had to explain to five different people that he was sure he put the vehicle in park before he got out. His colleagues gave him a hard time. "Hey, maybe a gremlin got in there and messed up the gears!" one of them said.

"Yeah, laugh it up," Mustache replied.

The arrival of the tow truck distracted the humans enough for Spark to sneak away. Once she made it back to the park, she pulled out the cellphone that Mason had given her and texted:

Children led me to hospital. Monsters have been in old wing!

A few seconds later, the phone buzzed.

Grand Sleuth checked hospital already. No monsters here. Stick 2 map we gave you. Find portal.

She could hear Mason's scolding voice as she read it. Though she expected another curt reply, she could not resist texting him again.

Keep an eye out @ hospital. Monsters are snooping around.

The phone buzzed again.

We R sending out regular patrols. Hospital safe. U do your job, we do ours. Time is short.

Spark wanted to smash the phone on the ground. These macho

Grand Sleuth bears were so intent on finding the portal, they were willing to ignore a threat right on their doorstep. Spark started typing a new text, which started with, "Listen, Mason."

But then she remembered Agnes pleading with her to be calm. The old bear had told her so many secrets. She answered all of Spark's questions. And she insisted that the children were safe. After all, Agnes's own dusa was at the hospital. The Grand Sleuth trusted Spark, and she needed to trust them in return.

Mumbling to herself, Spark deleted the new text. "You're still a jerk, Mason," she said.

She would deal with him later. For now, she needed to get home. Rather than sticking to the roads, Spark cut across the front lawns and backyards of the neighborhood. By taking the direct route, she made it home before the children. In the darkness of Loretta's room, Zed shivered in fear.

"It's okay," Spark said as she climbed up to her spot on the shelf. "They're safe. They're on their way back now." But Spark didn't feel as confident as she sounded. They now had two problems on their hands: the portal, and the children's curiosity.

Outside, a sharp wind slapped the tree branches against the window. Spark concentrated on Loretta, the way that Agnes had taught her. She imagined finding her somewhere, like a ship's captain spotting a lighthouse in the middle of a storm. Spark closed her eyes and tensed her body as she tried to focus.

"What's wrong?" Zed asked.

"Nothing."

That was it. She felt nothing.

Soon after, the back door opened. Loretta and Matthew tiptoed to their rooms. Loretta peeled off her jeans and hoodie, pulled on her pajamas, and flopped onto the bed.

In the morning, Dad called the children for breakfast. Neither of them stirred. Loretta snored while Mom and Dad made noise downstairs. Dad cranked the volume on the radio. Mom stacked plates in the dishwasher. When none of this worked, Dad switched on the garbage disposal. The grinding sound carried all the way to the second floor. Loretta pressed her pillow over her head and groaned.

Finally, Dad came stomping through the hall. "You told me your friends are getting here at eleven!"

Oh, that's right, Spark thought. Darcy, Jisha, and Claire were coming over to see the final cut of the movie.

This finally got Loretta moving, though she shambled about like a zombie. She and Matthew argued over who got to shower first. Matthew relented, so Loretta got in. After that, Loretta threw on her purple sweater and jeans. She pulled her hair into a bun and smeared on some lip gloss.

While the children ate, Mom and Dad peppered them with questions about how the movie turned out. Still exhausted, the children mostly mumbled their answers.

"How much sleep did you get last night?" Mom asked.

"I got enough," Matthew said.

"Hmm. Playing video games again."

Dad told Matthew that he needed to stop with video games after nine o'clock. Matthew retorted that he'd read an article saying that some people can operate on much less sleep than others. The parents did not fall for it. Mom told him she'd take his console away if his grades dropped like they did last year.

Loretta yawned, and Dad asked her why she looked so tired, too.

"Matthew's video games were too loud," she said, snickering.

"Oh, gimme a break!" Matthew said.

"I'm kidding," Loretta said. "Actually, uh . . . I'm working on a new script!"

"That's great!" Mom said. "What's it about?"

"Well, um . . . it's about people trying to solve a mystery. I don't know, it's stupid."

"That's not stupid," Dad said. "People love that stuff."

The doorbell interrupted them. To no one's surprise, always-punctual Darcy had arrived first. Though Spark could not see her from the shelf, she guessed that Darcy wore a dress, having come straight from church. Darcy and her bear Ozzie were so much alike. Darcy was kind, loyal, supportive. A listener who spoke only when it was necessary. While everyone said hello, Spark noticed the scent of something sweet.

"I brought you some banana bread," Darcy said. "My mom and I baked it this morning."

"Oh, we don't like banana bread," Dad joked.

Darcy paused. "Really?"

"Derek!" Mom said. "Don't listen to him, honey. He's gonna eat most of it."

The doorbell rang again and Matthew answered it. Jisha and Claire stepped inside, having run into each other on the way. Like her bear Lulu, Jisha was the talker in the group, the funny one. A smart aleck, according to her teachers.

Once everyone exchanged hellos, Jisha said, "We're winning this year. I'm calling it right now." She described how much better their movie was than the recent Oscar winner for Best Short Film, which she'd watched on YouTube the night before.

Claire changed the subject by describing the dress she planned to wear to the awards ceremony. She scrolled through images on her camera. Spark imagined her in the same flowing cape and shining armor that her Rana doll wore. Maybe she would wear a life-size version of Rana's crown as well.

The sound of all their voices made Spark think of the old days, when the girls were much younger. They would stomp all over the house, goofing around, while Mom and Dad made popcorn or cookies for them. They had sleepovers and game nights, class projects and movie marathons. All of those memories came rushing back to Spark, taking her mind off the frantic tension from the night before.

While they spoke, a car pulled into the driveway. "Sofia's here," Matthew said. Someone opened the door, and the room suddenly got quiet.

"Hi, Mr. Lopez," Matthew said. "Uh . . . where's Sofia?"

"Do you know where my daughter was last night?" Mr. Lopez asked.

"No?" Dad said.

"Ask your kids about it. Sofia came home at three in the morning. Covered in sweat and dirt. Doing God knows what. What kind of a house are you running over here?"

"Now, wait a minute—"

"And you girls," he said. Spark imagined him pointing to Loretta and the others. "You were there, too, I'll bet."

"What are you talking about?" Jisha said.

"Our kids were home," Mom said. But then she fell silent. Spark imagined her turning to Loretta and Matthew, putting the pieces together in her mind. The siblings were bad liars—their guilty faces gave them away.

"Ask them—they know," Mr. Lopez said. "I'm a single father. I work two jobs so I can keep my house in this neighborhood. It's hard enough to raise my daughter without your kids pulling this crap."

"Now, hold on—" Dad said, but Mom shushed him. Mr. Lopez needed to vent. No arguing would change that.

"I kept my promise to let Sofia make your little movie, but that's it," Mr. Lopez said. "It's over. Now stay away from us!"

The door slammed shut. Everyone remained completely still,

stunned. Spark could sense the parents' anger blooming in the silence. Darcy, Jisha, and Claire whispered to one another, wondering who knew what when.

Outside, the car sped away.

"Ladies, I'm sorry," Dad said. "We're gonna have to cut this short."

"I wasn't out last night," Jisha said.

"Let's go," Darcy said, no doubt pushing her friend toward the door.

"Text me," Claire said to Loretta.

"Bye, Claire," Dad said.

The girls hurried out. Judging from the scent, Darcy was nice enough to leave the banana bread behind.

"Family meeting," Mom said.

The children did not protest. They went to the kitchen, pulled out their chairs, and prepared to take their medicine.

FOURTEEN

Zed cried quietly while Mom and Dad talked to the children in the kitchen. "Is everything gonna be okay?" he asked.

Spark could not answer, so she climbed up to his shelf and put her arm around him.

Downstairs, Mom kept repeating the same thing. "What were you thinking?"

With no time to get their stories straight, the children couldn't lie. Yet the truth—or something close to it—sounded too crazy to say out loud. Mom and Dad had already told them about drugs, about strangers, about what websites they were allowed to visit on the internet. They'd given them a talk about how their bodies were changing after hearing that their Health class barely covered the topic. (This eventually devolved into a giggling fit for all four of them.) Because they'd been so open as parents, they never expected the kids to sneak around, especially at night.

"What if someone had gotten hurt?" Mom said.

"Were you showing off for Sofia?" Dad said.

"Oh, Dad, come on!"

"There are better ways to do that."

"I wasn't showing off!"

"Okay, fine, but we talked about this with Dr. Bannister," Dad said. That was Matthew's therapist. "Remember, she said this might happen. That you might start acting reckless."

"I'm fine. Nothing's 'happening,'" Matthew said.

"Is this the first time you guys did something like this?"

When Matthew didn't answer fast enough, Dad asked Loretta. "Of course," she said.

Then Dad started a long speech about how much trouble he would have been in if Grandpa had caught him sneaking out at night.

"Oh, man, this is bad," Zed said.

While the monkey whimpered, Spark thought of the man with the smile lurking in the window. It was unthinkable—a monster out in the open like that. And yet she had seen it with her own eyes. More monsters were following in Jakmal's footsteps, attracted to this town like sharks tasting blood in the water. If she didn't find that portal soon, something far worse might show up on her doorstep.

In the kitchen, Dad was asking why they had dragged Sofia into it. "Or was this her idea?" he asked.

Loretta insisted that the idea was hers, no one else's. But she stopped short of saying what they had really been doing. She must have realized that telling Dad what he wanted to hear—that they went out on a dare—would end the conversation faster. And spare everyone an emergency meeting with Dr. Bannister.

Spark could tell that the conversation would go on for a while.

"Zed," she said, "I know you're scared. But I need you to do something for me."

"What is it?"

"Get me Arctos. Then meet me at the bathroom window. Can you do that?"

"Arctos? What's wrong? Are we under attack?" Zed crouched into a fighting position—or what he thought a fighting position should look like—and scanned the room.

"I'm going to visit an old friend," Spark said. "I want to bring him something."

"An old . . . oh, you mean—"

"Yes."

"Right now? It's daytime!"

"Our family's occupied. And no one's home next door—the cars are gone."

"We should wait."

"Listen, Zed. If Sir Reginald is alive, he might know where that portal is. He was in Jakmal's castle, too. We can't wait. Now get the sword."

Together, they leapt from the shelf and went into the hall, where they split up. In the bathroom, Spark climbed onto the porcelain toilet tank. With all her might, she forced open the frosted window while trying not to let it squeak. Across the way was Jared's house. Right below the window, Mom's car sat in the driveway.

Zed rushed into the bathroom. "I got it," he whispered.

He joined her at the windowsill, where they scanned the yard and the street. No one was around, but that didn't stop Zed from grabbing her arm.

"Let's do this tonight," he said.

Spark pulled away from him. "Get ready to throw me the sword."

Like a diver, she bent her knees and leaned over the edge.

"No!" Zed said. "It's too high!"

"Zed, gimme a break, will you? I'm stuffed."

Spark jumped before he could object. Her fluffy belly hit the roof of the car with a soft *pat*. Then she rolled onto the driveway. She hopped to her feet again and waved to Zed.

"Quickly! The sword!"

Zed tossed Arctos, still in its scabbard and belt. When Spark caught it, it felt smaller than she remembered, like a kitchen utensil or a tool from the garage. It was never her sword. This weapon belonged to Sir Reginald.

"Now what?" Zed said.

"I find Sir Reginald," she said.

"But didn't he . . . die?"

"That's no excuse!" Spark replied. Which is exactly what Sir Reginald would have said.

Spark turned and headed for Jared's house. The window clicked shut behind her. Zed's form appeared behind the frosted glass. Spark could see him shaking his head at her latest crazy idea.

FIFTEEN

On Sundays, Jared's mom took him to his grandparents' house. This gave Spark some time to snoop around. She approached the doggie flap at the base of the kitchen door. Lucky for her, Jared's mom didn't have a dog anymore. Spark lifted the flap and peeked inside. The white tiled floor spread out toward a countertop and a humming refrigerator. The coast was clear.

This house had the same floorplan as Loretta's, but with newer furniture and a hardwood floor in the living room. Photos of Jared and his mom lined the mantelpiece. The images formed a timeline from left to right, from Jared's birth, to his class photos in kindergarten, to family vacations at the beach.

Spark's nose twitched at the scent of something familiar. Bear fur. Unmistakable. She got on all fours and followed the trail to the entrance of the den, where the carpet began. The scent became stronger in the fibers, stronger still in the cushy couch. At the other side of the room, next to the television, an enormous wooden chest overflowed with robots, NERF footballs, ray guns, and toy cars. Perhaps she would find Sir Reginald stuffed between a fire engine and a Frisbee.

As soon as she rose to her feet, she sensed a presence behind her.

"That's far enough," a macho voice said. Spark slowly turned. A police officer with a white motorcycle helmet flashed his badge at her. He was about six inches tall and made of plastic.

"Hands up," he said. "*Paws* up."

His shiny sunglasses created a funhouse reflection of the room. Spark recognized this toy. He was Officer Hogan, made by the same company that manufactured Rana, Amazon Princess™. Not as big a seller as Rana, but kids liked his battery-operated motorcycle and bank robbery playset, where Hogan would arrest Simon the Cat Burglar.

"State your business," the plastic cop said.

"I'm from the neighbor's house. I'm looking for a bear."

With his free hand, the cop reached for his walkie-talkie. "I'm going to have to call this in."

"No," she said, lowering her paws. "We're not doing this, okay? Your walkie-talkie doesn't work. I don't have time for this."

She thought he might listen to reason, but then he unhooked the handcuffs from his belt. "I need you to stay still."

"They won't fit," she said. "Stop it already."

Hogan lowered the cuffs, and his plastic lip quivered. He sniffed a little and then burst into uncontrollable sobbing. Louder than Zed on his worst day. "You're right! I'm a fraud!"

"Oh no," Spark said. She put her arm around him. He pushed her away at first. But then he gave in, and allowed her to console him. "Officer Hogan," she said. "*Bill*. Am I right?"

The cop sniffled. "Will."

"Sorry, Will. Listen. You're doing good work here. Take it from me. I'm from the League of Ursus. You've heard of us?"

"Yeah."

"I just need to know if there is a bear here. Black fur. Goes by the name of Sir Reginald. I need to know if he's like us. I mean, if he walks and talks."

The cop hung his handcuffs back on his belt. "*Sir* Reginald?"

Something moved in the toy chest. A soccer ball lifted and then rolled out, bouncing on the carpet. Two black ears and a pair of eyes rose over the edge. More toys spilled out as the bear climbed to the top of the pile.

It was Sir Reginald all right. Her friend really had returned from the final light! Now, in the toy chest, he looked like a mighty warrior on a mountaintop. A surge of pride and awe swept through Spark. This was the bear she remembered. The one who had trained her. Suddenly, the enormous task before her felt so simple. With Sir Reginald in her juro, she could do anything.

She spoke the words that Sir Reginald had used on the day he recruited her into the League of Ursus. "Bears serve. Bears watch. Bears protect. Always and forever."

"Oh, wow!" Sir Reginald shouted. He tumbled off the toy pile and skipped over to her. "Another teddy bear!" He bounced and clapped his paws, but stopped when Spark didn't join in. "How come you look so sad?"

His voice was different. He sounded like a child unwrapping a present.

"Trespasser," Hogan said, suddenly regaining the tone of a cop on the beat. "Must have had a troubled upbringing."

Sir Reginald tilted his head. "Is that true?" he asked. "Are you trespasser-ing?"

This must be an act, Spark thought. Sir Reginald had gone undercover to hide among these toys. Any second now, he would call her "Hotshot" to let her know that this was an act. To show how serious she was, Spark pulled out the sword. Sir Reginald flinched when he saw it.

"Drop the weapon!" Officer Hogan shouted.

Ignoring them both, Spark continued. "I am calling on all bears to be true. May you protect your dusa all through his days."

"You're funny!" he said. "Do you want to sing a song now?"

"A *song*?"

"Everybody loves songs! Come on. Clap your paws like this."

He patted his paws together in rhythm. One, one-two. One, one-two. Hogan joined in, his hands making a plasticky clicking sound.

This was not Sir Reginald. At least, it wasn't the bear she remembered.

"Ready?" he said. "This is one of Jared's favorites! Mommy says it was big in the eighties."

Spark stomped her foot. "Sir Reginald!"

The clapping stopped. The old bear lowered his snout. "My name's Reggie."

"No. It's Sir Reginald," said Spark. "And I need you to remember."

SIXTEEN

Spark had entered uncharted territory. A few weeks earlier, she thought that the final light was a throwaway line that League bears recited in their oath. "We defend the light—to the final light—in times of darkness." It sounded like some kind of nonsense that a bear must have mistranslated from the old days. And now, in this stranger's house, she tried to resurrect an old friend who had passed through the final light, from life to death and back again. He was a different bear now because he had a different dusa—a young, cheerful boy who loved songs and games. He was no longer the stern, no-nonsense warrior who had trained her.

Spark, Reggie, and Hogan sat in a triangle, like travelers gathering around a campfire. She told Reggie everything, from the day they met to the final battle with Jakmal.

"Oooh, I don't like scary stories," he said.

"It's not a story!" Spark said. "We really did this!"

"Mommy says that monsters aren't real."

"Mommy's usually right. This time she's wrong."

She pointed to his ankle. "If you look under the fur, you'll find some blue stitching. Am I right?"

Reggie ran a paw over his ankle. The fur lifted away, exposing a row of stitches. "How did you know that?"

"I sewed your foot back on after the monster attacked you. There's some stitching on your side, too."

He placed his paw there but did not examine any further.

Spark continued, all the way up to the moment where Matthew gave his old bear to Jared.

"Oh, right, Matthew," Reggie said. "The big kid next door!"

"The big kid, right. You used to be his bear. Now Jared is your dusa."

"You said that word before. What do you mean, *doo*-sah?"

"That's the child you're sworn to protect. Every bear has one."

Spark tried again to explain the League, the monsters, and how the Grand Sleuth had given her a mission of the utmost importance. Reggie nodded and smiled, and a small hope rose in her chest that he could somehow remember his old life. To further jog his memory, Spark walked the sword Arctos over to him. Holding the blade at eye level, she pointed at the various words carved into the metal in numerous languages.

"They all say the same thing," she said. "*Protector.* That's you. Here it is in Old English. Here it is in Latin—"

"Mommy said we're not allowed to play with knives."

"It's not a—" Spark stopped herself. She did not have time to debate the details. "Listen to me. You were in Jakmal's castle. You may have seen something. Some clue about where the last portal is. I need to find it or we're all in big trouble. You. Jared. Everybody. Do you understand?"

Reluctantly, the old bear—now a young bear—took the sword from her, holding it horizontally so that the blade nearly touched his snout. He sniffed it a few times. His eyes danced as he tried to read the alien words, the same word, carved again and again to remind him of his sacred duty.

"Is anything coming back?" Spark asked. "Anything at all?"

Rather than answer, Reggie decided to test the sharpness of the blade by poking the tip. He pulled his paw away and plugged it in his mouth like a child nursing a boo-boo.

Spark jangled the belt buckle. "Try it on. See if that rings a bell."

Reggie pulled the belt around his waist and tried to cinch it, only to find that his wide belly would not allow the buckle to close.

"I'm too chubby," he said, giggling. "I must have eaten too many cookies!"

"You have never eaten a cookie," Spark said.

Reggie glanced at Hogan to confirm this. Hogan shook his head no.

"When do we play League of Ursus?" Reggie asked.

Spark covered her eyes with her paws. "You don't *play* League of Ursus. League of Ursus is not a game."

"We could make it a game! And we could sing a song to go along with it."

Reggie and Hogan started clapping again.

"Stop it," Spark said.

"Just give it a try! You'll feel better."

Spark sighed. She turned to the window, toward the house that she needed to protect. For better or worse, the bear she once knew as Sir Reginald had adopted the traits of his new dusa. He was sweet. He was silly. Right now, that was exactly what Spark didn't need.

She grabbed his wrists to keep him from clapping.

"Hey!" he said.

"Can't you at least try? I need you, Sir Reginald."

The bear yanked his paws away and hugged himself. "My name's Reggie. And I don't like this game anymore."

With her eyes, Spark pleaded with Hogan for help. The officer glowered at her from behind his sunglasses. It meant one thing: she needed to leave.

"Keep the sword," she said to Reggie. "Hide it in a safe place. If you remember anything, come find me."

Spark headed for the doggie door. Though she wanted to cry, she held herself together. As she put her foot through the opening, she heard Hogan's boots clicking on the tiles. He stopped a few feet away.

"I'll talk to him," he said. "I know he used to be Matthew's bear."

"Thanks," she replied.

Back home, Spark peeked through the kitchen window. Inside, the family still sat around the table, hashing things out. Loretta and Matthew had both cried by this point, as had Mom. Spark could tell by their runny noses and red puffy eyes. They would be going at it for a little while longer, giving Spark some time.

The window in the living room was already open. She merely needed to lift the screen enough to squeeze through. At that moment, Dad was telling the children that maybe they shouldn't go to the film festival after all.

"*What?*" Matthew and Loretta both shouted at once. "That's not fair!"

"You guys think the rules don't apply to you."

"It was one time!" Matthew protested.

It went on like that while Spark pulled the screen back into place. There was no way they'd follow through on this threat, she thought. Maybe they would hold it over the kids for a few days, but they couldn't possibly take away the film competition.

Spark silently crossed the carpet while Mom explained—for probably the fifth or sixth time—that the children could talk to them. "You can tell us what you're thinking and feeling. You don't have to just run off like that!"

"Mom, we got it," Loretta said. She mumbled something, and

Mom demanded that she repeat it. By then, Spark had slipped past undetected.

Back in Loretta's room, Spark returned to the shelf and slumped into position.

"What happened?" Zed asked.

"Nothing. We resume the search tonight."

"Was Sir Reginald alive? I mean, was he . . . awake?"

Spark closed her eyes. It was too much. It was too hard to try to explain it all. "No," Spark lied. "He's still asleep."

SEVENTEEN

With the monsters closing in, the children's investigation halted, and no help coming from Sir Reginald, Spark needed to start over. Left on her own, she had little choice but to begin working her way through the map the Grand Sleuth had given her. There was so much ground to cover. The portal could be anywhere. But maybe, with Zed's help, she would get lucky.

In the old days, when Sir Reginald lived in Matthew's room, Spark would tap the closet wall three times every night at three a.m., and Sir Reginald would answer her from the other side. It was their signal that all was safe and sound. "Three at three," they called it.

With that in mind, Spark told Zed that they would "run at one."

"Whoa, whoa, whoa," Zed said. "Run at one?"

"We're going to run out of the house at one in the morning," Spark said.

The monkey squinted at her, like Loretta did when Dad told one of his jokes.

"I'm not good at coming up with cool rhymes, okay?" Spark said.

"Why does it have to rhyme?"

"Forget the name, okay? Just be ready at one."

To complete her mission, Spark needed to think like a monster.

So she asked herself: if I wanted to steal something from this world and then vanish without a trace, where would I place a portal?

When Spark asked Zed this question, the monkey responded with one of his own: "Well, what's out in the open but no one really looks at it?"

Spark thought about this while gazing out the window. And when the realization hit her, she covered her face with her paws. "The storm drains," she said.

"Oh no," Zed said. "No, no, no, no, no, no—"

While the family sat down for an awkward dinner, Spark unrolled the map and traced her paw along all the streets. Each block had at least five or six drains. She wondered if they might be too small for Jakmal, but the monster had proven to be very flexible, like an octopus squeezing through a tight space.

Zed kept going. "No, no, no. No way. There's no way, right?"

"Zed, be quiet for a second."

For once, Spark shared his fear. A few months earlier, Dad had shown the children a movie in which a monster reaches out of a storm drain and snatches a little boy in a yellow raincoat. Loretta usually loved scary movies, but halfway through she asked him to turn it off. Matthew made fun of her, but he was just hiding that he was scared, too. Thanks to that movie, Spark could easily imagine Jakmal's tail, with its pincer on the end, slithering out of the opening and dragging her into the darkness.

"Not going into a storm drain," Zed said. "No way."

"Maybe we won't have to," Spark said. "I'll figure something out."

Later that night, she did. The idea came to her while she stared at Mrs. Keller's yard across the street. A pile of white pebbles sat beside the garage. Any day now, a contractor would use them as the foundation of a new driveway. Spark needed a few dozen of the rocks, maybe a hundred—not enough for anyone to notice. Her plan made enough sense that even Zed agreed to give it a try.

So, that first night of Loretta and Matthew's grounding, Spark and Zed began their "run at one" by sneaking outside and putting on their uniforms. They stuffed their pockets with the stones until their jackets bulged. Under the buzzing streetlamps, Spark's shadow was lumpy with the extra weight. Beside her, Zed grunted with each step.

"Run at one," he said. "More like . . . waddle . . . at . . ."

"What does waddle rhyme with?" Spark asked.

"I'm working on it."

Zed mumbled a few other words, none of which worked.

"I got it," he said at last. "How about 'weigh a ton at one'?"

Spark repeated the phrase. "That's not bad."

The plan was to check every storm drain on the block. Zed was still nervous about being out in the open. No matter how many times Spark assured him that most humans were asleep, and couldn't see them in the dark anyway, he remained on high alert, his ears twitching and his eyes darting.

"Zed, focus," she said.

"I'm trying."

On opposite sides of the street, the first two storm drains waited for them, as ominous as the moat to Jakmal's castle.

Spark plucked a rock from her pocket. She gestured for Zed to do the same. They stood back-to-back in the street, each facing a drain. Spark went first. She rolled the stone across the asphalt and into the opening. A split second later, the stone clattered at the bottom. No portal. She turned to Zed. His hand shaking, the monkey tossed the stone and watched it disappear into the void. A clatter followed, and then an echoing *kerplunk* as the rock hit a puddle.

"Two down," Spark said.

Zed smiled.

"Two hundred to go," Spark added.

Zed lowered his tail.

"Come on," Spark said. "We're behind schedule. Let's get this done."

To keep Zed calm, she treated it like a game. They raced along the street, tossing the stones into each drain. Whenever a car passed, they took cover behind telephone poles or mailboxes. If anyone was bothering to listen at this time of night, they would have heard the chittering of stone on stone and then tiny footsteps scurrying away. Some healthy rats perhaps, nothing more.

They circled the entire block until they arrived where they'd started, at the pile in Mrs. Keller's driveway, now slightly smaller than before. Spark had planned it down to the last pebble, which she tossed into the drain in front of the Keller house. The familiar clatter echoed from the darkness.

"We did it!" Zed said. "Welp, no portals around here."

Spark turned to him. "We've ruled out one possibility. We now move on to the next."

This continued for the next few nights. At each sunrise, right before Loretta stirred from her sleep, Spark shaded in another area of the map. Along with checking the storm drains, they searched the golf course. The parking garage. The underpass—that was the worst for Zed because it was simultaneously dark and loud.

During that time, the children went to school, came home, ate dinner, and retreated to their rooms. After the big family meeting, they had little interest in talking. The tension would ease up at some point. For now, Mom and Dad let them be angry and mopey.

As part of the grounding, the parents took away the children's phones as soon they returned from school each day. Mom said they might enjoy the break, but Loretta and Matthew weren't buying it.

They still had their computers, which they were allowed to use only for homework. Still, Matthew managed to sneak in a video call to Sofia. Though Spark couldn't make out all the words, she could tell he was trying to apologize for talking her into joining their search.

"It's okay, it's okay," she replied. "It was my choice, too."

By the end, Spark could hear their stifled laughter—until Mom walked by Matthew's room and he cut the call short.

Loretta rewatched the footage from the movie, in which the man with the smile appeared like a mirage in the background, his skin as white and smooth as an egg. She expanded the image until his face occupied the entire window, pixelated and grainy.

A little box flashed at the bottom of the screen. It was Matthew messaging her.

"Wanna try again tonight?" he wrote.

Spark figured they were still debating what to do next, whether to continue their own search or not. Loretta ignored it at first. Soon, the messages piled on top of one another, with the last one reading, "R U gonna answer me???"

"Ugh," Loretta said. She typed, "Answer = no."

"We R already in trouble," he wrote. "Doesn't matter now."

She responded: "BTW I lost my swiss army knife the other night."

"Oh no! Let's go find it!"

"UR crazy."

With that, Loretta clicked the X at the top of the box and it disappeared.

EIGHTEEN

On Wednesday, Loretta came home from school at the usual time. Spark prepared for another boring day of her dusa being grounded. Loretta would finish her homework early and then mope around her room until dinner. After that, she would probably read in bed until she dozed off with a book propped on her chest. Then Spark and Zed would begin another search.

But instead of the usual routine, Loretta entered the room, lifted Spark from the shelf, and stuffed the bear into her backpack. The darkness sent Spark into a panic. Was Loretta running away from home? Was she chasing after monsters again, but this time all alone? And what would happen to Zed without her? Poor Zed. She had put him through so much these last few days. Spark's head spun with the possibilities. She bounced around in the backpack as Loretta trotted down the stairs.

Spark heard a car pulling into the driveway. Loretta carried Spark to the car and slid into the backseat.

"We're only doing half an hour, okay?" Mom's voice said.

Spark breathed a sigh of relief. So Loretta wasn't running away.

"That's fine," Loretta said.

"You're still technically grounded."

"How could I forget?" Loretta said.

The car backed out.

"Molly knows you're coming, right?" Mom said.

Oh, we're going to the hospital, Spark realized. Mom must have decided that Loretta's friendship with Molly was more important than Loretta being grounded.

"She knows," Loretta said. "Molly's mom works late on Thursdays, so she's stuck there alone."

"You brought your bear?"

Loretta patted the backpack. "She's here."

Spark had a feeling that Loretta didn't just want to see Molly or get out of the house for a little while. Loretta was still investigating, but this time in a quieter way.

At the hospital, Mom walked Loretta to the front desk to sign in as a visitor. The receptionists seemed thrilled to see her again.

"That's so nice of you to come visit your friend," a man said.

"Are you the one that gave Molly that poster?" a woman said. "The one for *Jason and the Argonauts*?"

"That's me," Loretta replied.

"I love that movie! You better bring Molly the DVD next time. She won't stop talking about it."

Loretta promised she would.

The same orderly from the other day led them to Molly's room. On the way there, Loretta unzipped the bag, pulled Spark out, and held her like a football against her chest.

When the orderly peeked inside Molly's door, he took a step back. "Good lord, what is going on in here?"

Molly had wedged a broomstick between the mattress and the frame at the end of her bed. The bedsheet was tied around it and unfurled all the way to the wall, like a sail. There was even a string attached to one end so it could be raised and lowered. Agnes sat at the front of the bed-ship. Molly stood behind her, using an empty paper towel tube as a telescope.

"Ya know, I thought you asked for the broom so you could sweep up and be helpful," the man said, laughing. "Now I know what you were really trying to do."

"The ship needed a mast," Molly said matter-of-factly.

Mom turned to Loretta. "I'm going to the grocery store," she said. "Back in thirty minutes."

"Got it," Loretta said.

"Try not to hit an iceberg," Mom said as she walked away.

Molly pointed at Spark. "You finally brought her!"

Loretta handed her the bear. Molly took Spark and held her at the waist for a closer inspection. "She's pretty old!" Molly said.

Spark tried not to feel insulted.

"Not that old," Loretta said. "Not as old as . . ."

"Agnes. I found her here. She's been at the hospital for a while."

Loretta nodded. "She's your first mate, and you're the captain?"

"Yeah. And you're the, uh, navigator."

"What should Spark be?"

"The cook."

The cook! Spark thought. She had never cooked so much as toast.

Molly plopped Spark next to Agnes. She took the biggest map from the wall, and it flopped on her head, covering her face and shoulders completely. Loretta giggled. Spark used the distraction to glance at the wall with all the drawings. There were no new pictures of the smiling man, which she took as a good sign.

Together, the two children flattened the map on the mattress. "Where should we go?" Molly asked.

Loretta ran her finger along the coast of South America, toward the Caribbean Islands. "How about here?"

Molly tried to read the words. "Trin. Na. Dad?"

"Trinidad. That's right."

"Greh-*nah*-da."

"Greh-*nay*-da," Loretta said.

"All right. Heave ho!" Molly pulled the string and the sail raised, blocking the window.

Wait, Spark thought. This was really happening. Her dusa, for the first time in years, was actually playing a game with her. After worrying about monsters for so long, Spark had stopped thinking of herself as a child's toy. But all of that fear melted away, replaced by the same joy she felt when Loretta would carry her around the house as a toddler, speaking her baby language and giggling the entire time.

And so they were off. Loretta did her best to play along. When a storm hit, Molly fluttered the sail and shook the boat. When a terrible sea creature emerged from the depths, Molly and Loretta speared it with a harpoon.

"He didn't die, though!" Molly said. "He went home and got stitches."

At one point, a huge wave swept Spark overboard, and Loretta dived into the ocean and saved her. Molly was so in character that she threw Loretta a rope—which was really the string from a yo-yo—and reeled her back to the boat.

"I've got you!" she shouted. "The sea will not take you yet!"

The little girl reminded Spark so much of Loretta when she was younger—a silly, lively, spirited child, filled with wonder, brimming with laughter.

Later, the ship ran aground off the coast of a mysterious island. Agnes bravely volunteered to explore first—to make sure that it was safe. Molly walked her around the room, inspecting under the chair and out the window and behind the bed.

"Is that what Agnes does for you?" Loretta said. "She keeps an eye out for danger?"

Molly stopped and thought about it. "Yeah. Does Spark do that, too?"

"Sure."

Molly plopped Agnes next to Spark on the bed, so that the two bears faced each other. *Wait, what are we doing?* Spark thought. *Let's keep playing!*

"You said you were too old for a teddy bear," Molly said.

"Well, too old to play with her. But I still keep her close to me."

No, you're not too old, Spark thought.

"Did you used to play pirates with Spark?"

"Hmm . . . not pirates. But we had other adventures. One time . . ."

Loretta started laughing. Spark knew exactly the story she was about to tell.

"I used to take her to my Grandma's," Loretta said. "One year, on the Fourth of July, I snuck out while everyone was cooking dinner and got lost in the woods behind her house."

Molly gasped.

"The sun went down," Loretta said, "and I was so scared. I couldn't see anything. And the crickets were so loud. I can still hear them." She did her best imitation of a cricket sound.

Loretta lifted Spark at the neck. "I cried the whole time. But I held Spark like this, and she made me feel safer. And not alone. When they found me later that night, I wouldn't let go of her. And I remember there was this, like, handprint on her fur, 'cause my palm was so sweaty and I'd held her so tight."

Spark remembered it well. It was gross.

"You know, I snuck out again the other night," Loretta said, putting Spark down.

"Did Spark go with you?"

Loretta laughed. "No. But I guess I should have brought her. I got in big trouble when my parents found out."

Loretta went to the window and looked out at the abandoned hospital wing. "I told you that something happened to my brother. How he went missing for a few days. Remember?"

"Yeah."

Spark snapped out of her playful mood. This was getting serious.

"Ever since then, I think we've all been seeing the same . . . monsters." Loretta had trouble getting the word out. Everyone else laughed when they heard that word, but this little girl would understand.

"Like these?" Molly said, pointing at her drawings.

"No. Like the one you showed me the other day. The bald guy. Where is it?"

"I threw it out. I didn't want my mom to see."

"Have you . . . have you seen him again?"

Molly brushed a piece of lint from her robe. "No."

"You're sure?" Loretta sounded desperate.

Molly looked at the floor and nodded.

"Because we went looking for him. In the old wing of the hospital."

"Really?" Molly asked. "Why would you do that?"

"I don't even know anymore. I just know that something weird is going on. The adults wouldn't listen to us. So we just . . . We were trying to prove something. Prove we weren't scared, I guess."

"Were you?"

"Yeah! I mean, look at that place! It's creepy!"

Molly giggled. During the daytime, the old wing looked more sad than scary.

"You were with your friends, though," Molly said.

"Yeah," Loretta said. "That made me feel . . ."

"Safe?" Molly said.

"Yeah," Loretta said. "Stronger. Like the time . . ."

Her voice trailed off, but Spark knew what she was thinking. Loretta was remembering the time she opened a portal in order to save Spark. Her friends were all there with her. Their presence helped Loretta do it. Somehow. It was as good an explanation as any.

"Can Spark stay here with me?" Molly asked. "She'd make me feel safer. And stronger."

"I'll bring her back to visit, but I need her this week," Loretta said. "For the film festival."

Loretta explained that the festival was going to display props from the competing movies in an exhibit hall. She'd hoped to show off all the stars of her movie—Spark, Zed, Ozzie, Lulu, and Rana. "I'm not sure yet if my parents will let me go, though," she said. "Still grounded."

"I wanna see your movie!"

"Ask your mom. Maybe she can bring you to the premiere."

While they talked, Spark and Agnes finally had the chance to whisper to each other.

"Quickly," Agnes said. "Give me an update."

"No luck," Spark said. "Looked almost everywhere."

"You wasted a night coming here, I'm told."

"I had to follow the children. But I could tell there were monsters in the empty wing. I could smell them!"

Agnes sighed. "We've been over this. The hospital is safe."

"But Molly says she saw something."

"She can see things in her dreams. Things that haven't happened yet."

"But things that *could* happen! Like the monsters attacking the hospital."

"Yes!" Agnes said curtly. "Which is exactly why we need you to stick to the plan."

Agnes had never snapped at her like this.

"I appreciate your passion," Agnes said more calmly. "But time is running out. We gave you a job to do."

Spark had no choice but to drop it. "You're right. I'll stick to the plan. We're almost done with the map."

"I like your dusa," Agnes said.

"I like yours," Spark replied.

Someone knocked on the door. It was Mom, already back from the grocery store. "Are you ready?"

"You said thirty minutes!" Molly whined.

"It's been thirty-three," Mom replied.

"I'll be back," Loretta said to Molly. "And I'll bring Spark again, okay?"

While they said their goodbyes, Agnes managed to sneak in one more whisper, so quiet that Spark barely heard it.

"Find that portal," she said. "Everything depends on it!"

Loretta shoved her bear into the backpack. Everything went dark again.

"Bye, Spark!" Molly said.

Spark waved goodbye from inside the backpack. She hoped Loretta would visit Molly again soon. She wouldn't mind being the ship's cook.

For now, she had a job to do. If she was ever going to enjoy another day like this one, where she could forget all the things that scared her, then she needed to complete her mission. For Loretta. And for Molly.

NINETEEN

That night, Spark and Zed once again met at the spot behind the bushes. Spark pulled the plastic bag from under the dirt where it hid. By now, the soldier outfits looked like they'd survived a real war, all stained with soil and dotted with holes on the knees and elbows. She handed Zed his outfit. He took it but did not put it on. Instead, he laid it flat in front of him, as if it were the skin of a dead animal.

"What's wrong?" Spark asked.

Zed tilted his head. "What's wrong? We've been at this for days. Either the portal isn't out there, or it's in a place we can't find."

"You want to give up?"

"Yes! I mean no. I want us to come up with a better plan."

"Well, I want a pony for Christmas." (Dad always said this whenever the kids whined about not getting something they wanted.)

"Do you have a better plan?" Zed asked.

"No. Do you?"

"Why don't you go back to the Grand Sleuth and tell them we can't find it? Tell them to bring in reinforcements?"

"Zed, there are no reinforcements. I told you that. *We're* the reinforcements."

The monkey walked away, toward Jared's house. "I really tried to do this with you. I wasn't made for this."

"That's right. You weren't."

She carried his helmet to him. He wouldn't take it.

"You're *choosing* to do this," Spark said. "You're choosing to do the thing that you weren't meant to do. Because it's the right thing to do."

"No, no, you're giving me a speech. No more speeches. No more oaths. I can't do this. What if we get caught? We're only making things worse!"

"The children are searching. We should search, too."

"No, we—it's different, okay?"

"How is it different?"

"Stop it! You're trying to confuse me!" He hopped about the yard like a bunny. The movement triggered the security light. Suddenly, the grass and the driveway were bright as day. One of the lights stretched Zed's bouncing shadow all the way to the street. The other projected it onto the wall of Jared's house.

"How 'bout this, how 'bout this," he said, talking faster. "How about we find a pay phone. Do they still have pay phones? Find a pay phone, place a call to the police. Place a . . . hieronymus tip."

On the wall of Jared's house, Spark noticed a dark spot above Zed's shadow, like a burn mark. She rubbed her eyes, thinking the brightness was playing tricks on her.

Zed kept fighting with the word. "Hieronymus. Anomynous? Whatever."

"Zed, shush for a second."

"They have people who investigate ghosts and monsters, you know. I saw them on TV. They can help!"

"Quiet!" she said. "Look!" Spark pointed.

On the wall of Jared's house, under the windowsill, was a tight row of smudge marks. From a distance, the markings looked like a collection of dirt, or a shadow, or a bloom of mold. But as Spark got closer, she noticed a distinct pattern.

Bears sometimes put markings on the outside of their houses to alert other bears of danger in the area. Like ancient Egyptian hieroglyphs. Typically, the marks consisted of a trio of paw prints, the signal for help. Spark had tried this very tactic when Jakmal first appeared. But in this case, the symbols traveled all the way across the window frame, scrawled with ashes—perhaps from a cigar—so that the next rain would wash them away.

"What is that?" Zed said.

Spark recognized the first few symbols. A simple arrow pointing north, followed by a paw print, then the letter X inside a square.

"Wait! I know what this is!" Zed said. "A bear drew this! A bear from the League of Ursus!"

A long time ago, Sir Reginald taught this language to Spark. (Zed had asked to learn, too, but got bored after the first lesson and quit.)

"Can you read it?" Zed asked.

"I think so. Arrow points north. One paw print after the arrow means one mile. Then the X. The X means danger."

"A monster?"

"It's the portal. Reggie must have remembered where it is."

"Who's Reggie?"

Spark quickly filled in Zed about what really happened to Sir Reginald. "When I said he was still asleep, I didn't mean that he was dead," she said. "Just that he didn't remember us."

Zed stared at her for a second. "You lied."

Spark looked at the ground. "I thought I had to. Maybe I didn't. I'm sorry."

"I can handle the truth, you know," Zed said. "Sometimes."

An awkward silence followed. Zed faced the house again and pretended to read the symbols. "He must have remembered Matthew at least?" he said.

Spark shook her head no. "It was like he was a completely different bear."

"Would I be a different monkey if someone else took me away?"

"I suppose you would. But if you didn't remember your old life, I guess you wouldn't miss it."

"That's awful!"

Spark would have to ponder this later. Right now, she needed to translate the rest of the symbols. After the X was a horseshoe shape with a pair of wings next to it. Then a triangle with a line through the middle. Then a square with another triangle on top. At the very end of the row, barely visible, was a symbol that made no sense: an arrow that looped down and then back up again.

"Okay, the triangle is a hill," Spark said. "The square with a triangle on top is a house. But the horseshoe and the wings . . . I don't know. Could mean a barn. And the wings . . ."

"I got it!" Zed said. "A barn that can fly!"

"Be serious, Zed!"

Zed's tail drooped. "I was being serious," he muttered.

Spark squinted at the symbols. She tilted her head until the horseshoe tipped over on its side.

"Oh no," she said, unfolding her map. "Please, no."

"What is it?"

Spark flattened the map on the grass and traced her paw from the house to the north. There, another grassy area had been shaded in. Close to the hospital. The Grand Sleuth had already checked it and found nothing. But Sir Reginald's message said otherwise.

"Is that another park?" Zed asked, trembling.

"Sort of. I don't think the bears have a word for it. Reggie had to improvise."

"So the wings . . ."

"The wings represent angels," Spark said. "And the horseshoe is a tombstone."

"So the park . . ."

"Is a cemetery."

"Are you sure?" Zed said desperately. "Lemme see the map. That can't be right."

"I just *know* there were monsters at the hospital," Spark said. "No matter what the Grand Sleuth says. Maybe the monsters plan to attack from the cemetery before anyone notices."

Zed let out a defeated sigh.

"Don't you see what this means?" Spark said. "It means the kids were on to something. They knew something wasn't right! It's amazing."

"Sure, amazing."

Zed swooned, then fell flat onto his back, his arms and legs splayed out. "Of course. Of course it's in the cemetery."

"You fought off Jakmal and now you're afraid of ghosts?"

"I'm afraid of traps. This is a trap."

"You say that about everything."

"This time I'm right! Besides, the Grand Sleuth didn't even ask us to search there. They already did."

"They must have missed something. When Sir Reginald was in Jakmal's castle looking for Matthew, he must have opened a door that took him there. He would know better than anyone else."

Spark figured that the house symbol meant a building inside the cemetery. The triangle meant a hill. A building on a hill in the cemetery. Simple enough.

There was still the looping arrow to translate. It could be telling her to go back the way she came, or it could mean that something was upside down. She imagined Sir Reginald scolding her for not getting it. "This is another test, Hotshot," he would say. "What good is your strength if your mind fails you?" Spark would have to figure it out after she got there.

"All right, I have good news and bad news," she said.

Still on his back, Zed eyed her suspiciously.

"Good news is that you don't have to go to the cemetery."

"And the bad news?"

"If I don't return by sunrise, you have to get to the hospital. Tell the Grand Sleuth what happened. They'll take it from there."

Zed wrung his hands. "Oh, all right."

Spark checked her equipment. She carried a flashlight, a map, her sword, and the cellphone the Grand Sleuth had given her. The moment she found this portal, she would text them and then get out of there.

Before she left, she placed her paw on the symbols and rubbed until they blurred into a dark smudge.

"Thank you, Reggie," she whispered.

TWENTY

By now, Spark had grown accustomed to the eerie quiet of the neighborhood after midnight. If things went according to plan and the Grand Sleuth could close the last portal, then this mission would come to an end. She realized that for all the trouble these expeditions caused, she would miss them. It was strange how something once so frightening, so impossible, had become routine. That was the freedom one could enjoy after overcoming a fear. Maybe that's what it felt like to grow up, though Spark imagined she would discover more fears—and have to summon more courage to conquer them.

A fog bank rolled across the neighborhood, cloaking the streetlamps and traffic lights in a strange aura. Only one vehicle passed by: a delivery truck driven by a sleepy, bearded man, his face illuminated by the dashboard. Spark didn't bother hiding; the man's eyes were on the road.

After many silent blocks, she reached a dead end at the stone wall that marked the edge of the cemetery. Unable to climb over, she headed for the arched gate, where a chain and padlock secured the entrance. She shimmied underneath. Once on the other side, she surveyed the landscape. A single road weaved through the graveyard, illuminated by old streetlamps. The headstones formed neat rows all the way up the hill at the center, like columns of soldiers. Off to the side, a clutch of dying trees loomed over the older headstones. These markers were smaller than the others, like little loaves of bread, and more tightly packed together.

Reggie's message must have referred to the hilltop where a group of mausoleums housed the remains of the richest families in town. Spark followed the road all the way up the hill. The mausoleums resembled little houses made of stone, with crosses on their triangular rooftops. In the middle stood the largest one, right beside the oldest tree in the cemetery. Its roots had grown so far that they tilted the stone structure. There were two angels carved into the pillars in front. The word WILSON was etched above the double doors.

Spark grasped the huge metal doorknob and pulled herself up to the glass window. After brushing away the dust, she shined her flashlight inside. Marble walls divided the narrow space into chambers where the Wilsons rested. Each tomb had a name and a lifespan carved into the surface.

Spark remembered the final symbol in Reggie's message—the curved arrow that signified something being upside down. She tilted the flashlight to the ceiling, but nothing appeared out of place. No scratches on the walls, no footprints. No loose tiles on the floor. No hints that someone may have opened or closed this door.

Spark dropped from the knob and backed away to get a wider look. "Come on, Wilson, help me out here," she said.

A walk around the outside of the building did not help. Grass stalks grew tall where the groundskeeper's lawnmower couldn't reach. As she completed a full revolution, she had the terrible feeling that Reggie had simply written the first gibberish that came to mind. A kind of mental muscle memory.

The tree yielded no clues, either. Leaf buds had begun to sprout on the dormant branches, ready to burst open in the springtime. Two of the sturdier branches hung over the mausoleum like outstretched arms, growing out of a thick knot on the trunk. There, a hawk or some other bird of prey had built a large nest out of twigs and leaves, at least three feet wide. It looked abandoned, at least for the season.

Spark figured she could survey the area from there. As she climbed, a fog drifted across the cemetery, leaving only the top of the hill exposed. On reaching the nest, she marveled at its perfectly round shape, like a baby's crib. Fragments of eggshell stuck to the bottom, alongside a pile of dried mouse bones. Spark hopped into the nest and leaned over the side, shining her flashlight on the mausoleum. As the beam swept across the roof, an imperfection in the stone caught her eye. The portal? No. These were grooves scratched into the rock. Claw marks. Much too large for a bird, too wide for a canine or even a bear. Jakmal had stood there. In fact, he had landed there from some great height.

A wave of panic shivered through her. Spark squeezed the flashlight as she waited for the feeling to pass. Before she could change her mind, she swung her body over the branch and dangled from it. The underside of the nest seemed unnaturally flat. She pointed her flashlight at it and the beam simply vanished as if swallowed by a black hole. A hint of grease and soot—the stench of Jakmal's world—tickled her nose.

"No," she said slowly.

When she extended her paw, her arm disappeared all the way to her shoulder. She yanked it out, stuck it in, then yanked it out again. A giddy wave of joy overtook her. Here was her portal! Suspended in midair, right under the bird's nest! And it was upside down, just like Reggie said. Though it was small, Spark knew firsthand how a portal could expand to fit anything, including a monster.

She needed to know for sure that this was Jakmal's portal and not some other monster's. Before she had time to feel afraid, Spark holstered the flashlight and lifted herself into the blackness. Everything in her field of vision spun around. Her paw pressed onto a cold cobblestone floor. Somehow, the surface was both vertical and horizontal at the same time. She pushed herself all the way through until she flopped face-first on the ground.

Disoriented and trembling, Spark stood and unsheathed her sword. She was in the hallway of Jakmal's castle! She turned in a circle, pointing the blade outward from her chest. No one was around.

Torches burned on the walls, their black smoke staining the vaulted ceilings. In one direction, the hall ended at the castle's main gate, which was sealed shut by a wooden drawbridge. In the other direction, the hall continued infinitely, vanishing to a tiny point. The fortress possessed a special magic, allowing it to house doorways to other worlds. Spark had once asked Sir Reginald where the doors went. "Everywhere," he said.

Something was different, though. Several of the torches were extinguished, leaving sections of the hall in darkness. A few lay on the floor amid piles of ash. When a loose pebble fell down and pinged off her helmet, Spark noticed an enormous crack in the ceiling. It spread all the way to the drawbridge, as if damaged by an earthquake. Or a volcanic eruption. After all, the castle was built into the side of a volcano. Or maybe Jakmal went berserk after his defeat. He must have raged and thrashed until he could barely stand, destroying his own home in the process.

Spark had seen enough. She turned back the way she came. On this side, the portal was an arched entrance, with its wooden door hanging open. Impossibly, like an optical illusion, the portal directly faced the roof of the mausoleum. This is what Sir Reginald saw when he went searching for Matthew in the castle. In his desperation to track down his dusa, he found himself hanging above the Wilson family's tomb—a vivid memory that lasted even beyond the final light.

When Spark stuck her paw through the door, she felt gravity shift, tugging her arm away from her. She tested it, pushing her arm farther each time. Realizing too late that she had leaned too far, she slipped and plummeted through the opening, bounced off the mausoleum roof, and landed in the grass. Her helmet rolled away and spun to a stop. Her sword landed blade first in the ground.

Spark sat up, looked around. No one was there to see her little accident. A light feeling began in her tummy, rising until it burst forth in a fit of laughter. All the tension of the last few days emptied out of her.

She pulled out the phone. As she typed a message to the Grand Sleuth, she imagined the look on Mason's face when he saw that she had passed another of his tests, one that he had failed. She decided not to rub it in. She would not gloat. Finding the portal and acting like she never doubted herself would be more satisfying.

Cemetery on Huey Avenue, she typed. Wilson mausoleum in the middle of the graveyard. Come find me!

TWENTY-ONE

While sitting between the two angel statues that guarded the tomb, Spark turned the phone over in her paw. After a few minutes, she sent the message again. If nothing else, perhaps repeating it would get on Mason's nerves.

The wind blew away the fog, though the grass remained cold and wet. Leaves rustled in the breeze. The sound made Spark nervous, so she decided to wait among the older tombstones in case Jakmal—or anything else—decided to make an appearance.

She hid behind the tombstone of a David Harper, whose marker showed the death date of June 2, 1918. Beside him was Sarah Harper, his wife, who died in 1922. That was only a few years after teddy bears began to be mass produced, and the League gained the upper hand against the monsters. The Parkers' children had grown up in a world where monsters were on the run. And to think that such a hard-won victory was now threatened. The League would have to push the monsters back again, one portal at a time. Spark's mission had grown beyond the protection of one child, a situation Sir Reginald could never have predicted during her training.

She tried to think of something else, something from a simpler time. As she fished through her memories of Loretta's early birthday parties, a large raccoon scurried by, startling her. The raccoon stopped and rose on its hind legs, sniffing around the doorframe of the mausoleum. Another raccoon waddled over. Now both of them were inspecting the door.

"Hmm," Spark murmured.

Next, a stray cat with an abnormally large belly arrived. Spark figured she must be ready to give birth to a litter of kittens. Instead of picking a fight with the raccoons, the cat acknowledged their presence and then sniffed the grass along the building.

A skunk ambled in their direction, its fluffy tail bopping with each step.

"What is going on?" Spark whispered.

The skunk stood on its hind legs and gripped its neck. With a horrifying *snap!*, its head popped off. Spark covered her mouth to keep from screaming. The raccoons and the cat seemed completely unfazed.

Then a furry face emerged from the hole in its neck.

"Where is the teddy bear?" the headless skunk said. Spark recognized the voice. It was Mason!

She emerged from behind the tombstone. "Over here!"

All the animals suddenly stood up like children who've been caught playing some odd game. Each pulled off their own mask. A purple bear with a round face wore one of the raccoon costumes. Iggy, the polar bear, removed the cat mask and straightened his red Santa hat underneath. He must have been the one who designed the costumes. His best work yet! More disguised bears arrived. Mostly raccoons, but also a fox, a groundhog, and a very fat squirrel.

"I'm glad you're here," Spark said to Mason. "You won't believe what I went through—"

"Where's the portal?" Mason said impatiently.

"Mason, please," Iggy said. Turning to Spark, he said, "Forgive my friend. He gets to the point so quickly sometimes that he forgets how sharp it can be."

"The portal, please," Mason said.

"There," Spark said, pointing to the nest.

Mason searched the ground until he found a small stone. Positioning himself under the nest, he tossed the rock underhand and watched it vanish. A second later, it fell into his palm again. "Clever," he said.

Spark nodded. "Yes. This monster knows how to—"

"I was talking about you," Mason said coldly.

Iggy chuckled. "Did you just give our new friend a compliment?"

With his paws on his hips, Mason kept his gaze on the portal. "She did it."

Spark would take it. As she allowed herself to smile, Iggy began clapping his soft paws. Soon, all the bears joined in. Mason joined last. A few bears showed their appreciation by giving Spark a playful shove or a hard pat on the shoulder.

Everyone suddenly fell quiet as two large bears pushed their way through the crowd. The oversized bodyguards stood aside, allowing Agnes to hobble forward. She leaned heavily on her cane.

"Agnes!" Iggy said. "What are you doing here?" He raced over to help her walk, but she shooed him away.

"Changed my mind," she said. "I needed to see it for myself. And I am *not* going to issue orders from our sanctuary. I may not move as fast as some of you, but we're in this together."

The bears nodded. She was their general, risking herself alongside them.

"Now," Agnes said, "where is the cub?"

Iggy gestured toward Spark. As the pink bear approached, Spark again noted her stitching, the dullness of her fur, the worn patches on her knees and elbows, and she felt a sense of awe at the elderly bear's age and experience. Agnes took Spark's paw and led her away from the crowd.

"Thirty minutes," Agnes called over her shoulder. "Then we head back."

"What are they doing?" Spark asked.

"They are running tests on the portal. We're still trying to learn how they work."

She squeezed Spark's paw and gave her a wistful look, the same one Sir Reginald had while talking about his adventures in the old days, when Dad was his dusa and the world was so much smaller.

"Let the scientists handle it," Agnes said. "For now, I want you to tell me all about how you got here. You have had the kind of adventure that we hear about only in our legends and myths."

"Well," Spark said, "I don't know if it's worthy of a legend."

"Let's find out," Agnes said. "Tell me your story of bravery and honor, so I can feel like a cub again."

TWENTY-TWO

While the sky turned brighter in the east, the Grand Sleuth gathered around the old tree. Spark and Agnes sat on a tombstone and watched as the bears erected a tripod, which held a digital tablet. Mason tapped on the screen while Iggy pointed a device at the portal. It resembled a microphone, connected by a wire to a metal box. Like a Geiger counter. Spark assumed that the portal gave off some kind of energy that only special machines could detect. She had heard of warrior teddy bears, but scientist bears like Mason were new to her. Then again, Sir Reginald would have said there's room for all types in the League.

Agnes pinched the sleeve of Spark's camouflage jacket. "You remind me of a G.I. Joe doll we had at the hospital."

"You should see Zed in this outfit," Spark said. "Hey, where's *your* disguise?"

Agnes pointed to a hunk of black plastic attached to her shoulder. "I have a little string that I pull on and *poof!* A trash bag shoots out. I lie beneath it and wait for the danger to pass."

"What if someone picks you up and tries to put you in the garbage?"

"It's happened only once. I thrashed around, and he dropped me and ran away. Probably thought I was a rat."

While they spoke, Iggy called out the readings from the device. "Point seven five," he said.

Mason keyed the information into the tablet. "Point seven five," he huffed. The number disappointed him somehow.

"Aren't you afraid that a monster might come through the portal?" Spark asked.

"Of course. That's why we brought some muscle." She explained that Jakmal, at that very moment, might be waiting on the other side, sniffing for bears. He would realize that he was outnumbered this time. "He poked the hornet's nest," Agnes said.

Despite these reassurances, Spark couldn't help but glance around nervously.

"And we won't be discovered by any humans, either," Agnes assured her. "We have lookouts covering a half-mile radius. This is no amateur hour."

"Have you given any thought to how we might help Jakmal break his curse?"

"We put out a call," Agnes said. "There are bears who can help. Hexens. I've known them for a long time. They're on their way and they will advise us on what to do next."

Under the tree, Iggy continued tinkering with the Geiger counter. "Holding at zero point seven," he said.

"Have these hexens ever done anything like this before?" Spark said.

"No." Agnes said. "As far as I know, Jakmal is the only one of his kind."

Agnes asked how Loretta was doing. "She's busy with her own investigation," Spark said. "I'm worried she's going to get in trouble again."

"She will," Agnes said. "That's part of the deal. All children are special in their own way. And they will find their own destinies, with or without our permission."

Agnes shifted her large behind on the tombstone. "You may find more answers by connecting with your dusa. Like I taught you. Have you tried it?"

"I have. I don't think I can do it."

"It *will* work," Agnes said. "Just remember that the child possesses the power, not the bear. We are mere extensions of their minds. Next time, let her do the work."

Mason walked over to Agnes. Behind him, the other bears began to dismantle the tripod. "Readings check out," he said. "Just as we predicted."

"So you can make it work," Agnes said.

"It will take some time. But we have the data we need."

Two bears carried the tripod to Mason. One of them pointed to a screw holding the tablet in place. Mason dug inside his costume and pulled out a Swiss army knife. With a green handle. *Loretta's* knife.

Spark remembered Loretta telling Matthew that she lost the knife in the abandoned wing of the hospital. Now she tried to maintain a neutral expression while her mind raced through the possibilities. Had the Grand Sleuth gone snooping there as well? After all their assurances that it was monster-free? Why hadn't they told her?

Had they been . . . watching her?

While Mason opened the knife's screwdriver, Agnes chattered on about Molly. How her friends missed her, how her class sent her pictures and letters.

"Sure," Spark said, still looking at the knife.

After a few turns, the screw came loose. Mason caught the tablet before it fell. The bears took the tripod away, and Mason retracted the screwdriver.

Spark chose her next words carefully. "So, when do we destroy the portal?"

Iggy looked at Mason. Mason looked at Agnes.

"I mean, that's why we're here, isn't it?" Spark said.

"Now that we are done with our tests, we will leave behind a small group," Agnes said. "They will take care of it."

"Can I watch?"

Again, Mason looked at Agnes.

"I've never seen it before," Spark added. "How does it work?"

"You could watch," Agnes said. "I would not try to stop you. But you know that we have been out in the open for quite some time. It is probably best we return."

Agnes was trying to get her to agree in the most subtle way possible—by appealing to her sense of honor and her obedience to the rules.

"You're right," Spark said. The relief on Agnes's face told her everything she needed to know.

"You should head home," Agnes said. "We will call on you again soon."

"You mean when the hexens arrive?"

Agnes eyed her.

"I'd love to meet them."

"Of course," Agnes said. "We can contact you—"

"What are their names, by the way?"

"What?"

"Their names," Spark said. "You told me you've known them for years."

Agnes gripped the handle of her cane a little tighter. "Their names . . . change, of course. They go under an alias."

Agnes had an answer for everything. And yet she dodged the simplest question Spark could have asked.

"Spark, we need to move along," Agnes said. "When this task is over, we can complete your training. Assuming you still want to join us and take your place on the Grand Sleuth."

"Sounds great," Spark said. She noticed Mason watching her. "Hey, can I see your knife?" she asked. "Uh, please?"

Mason cast another glance at Agnes. The old bear nodded, and he handed the knife to Spark.

"I need to get one of these," Spark said.

"Ah, yes. Very useful," Mason said.

By this point, more bears had gathered around.

"How come *she* gets to hold it?" one of the bears said.

"She asked nicely," Mason replied.

Spark flipped the knife to find two letters carved into the handle. *LR*. Loretta's initials.

"Where did you get this?" sheh asked.

"One of the doctors left it behind when he transferred to another hospital."

An utter lie. No way around it. This was the same bear who had sent her that angry text message, insisting there were no monsters at the hospital. Almost as if he was daring her to call him a liar.

"Oh, and it has a little toothpick," Spark said.

"Yes!" Despite his no-nonsense attitude, Mason had an almost childlike enthusiasm for gadgets. "The tweezers are not very good," he noted. "Though we did use them to extract a splinter from Bradley's foot."

"He acted like it hurt," Iggy said.

A chubby bear with black fur pushed his way into the conversation. He must have been Bradley. "This again," he huffed. "*You* try getting stabbed through the foot!"

"Stabbed? It was a splinter!" Iggy said.

"Technically speaking, you do not have nerve endings," Mason said.

"Yeah, well, it felt like I did."

"Without nerve endings, you cannot *feel* anything. That is my point."

"Hey, do you mind if I try something?" Spark said.

She retracted all the tools in the knife except one: the blade, which was almost as large as the sword Arctos. "How much do you wanna bet I can hit that tree over there?"

"This is not a throwing knife," Mason said.

"Oh, it will be." The tree was at least twenty yards away. Spark pointed to a knot on the trunk about three feet from the ground. "That knot there. I could hit that."

The bears broke into a dispute over whether it was possible. While they argued, Spark glanced at the tablet, which the bears had set on top of the dismantled tripod. The screen displayed a diagram of the portal, with a row of fluctuating numbers beside it. Just running some tests on the portal, Agnes had said. What were they *really* up to?

"After this silly game is over, we go back," Agnes said. Her words silenced everyone.

Spark spread her arms so that the crowd would give her room. She twirled the knife as she calculated the distance. "These are the skills you'll need if the monsters ever come back to the hospital," she said.

"They won't—" Mason said, but stopped himself. "They've never made it to the hospital."

The way the bears looked at him, pleading with him to get the story right—Spark knew then that every last one of them was hiding something.

She would continue pretending otherwise for a few more seconds. Holding the knife by the blade, she threw it so that it flipped end over end toward its target. When the bears turned to watch it fly,

Spark spun around and grabbed the tablet. She ran away into the darkness, where the tombstones would provide obstacles to anyone who tried to chase her.

"She took it!" someone shouted.

As Spark zigzagged around the stones, one of them appeared to move on its own, blocking her path. She collided with the soft belly of a bear and nearly fell over.

It was Mason. And somehow he was holding Loretta's knife!

Spark reeled from the sight of him. "What the . . ."

She turned and ran along another row of tombstones. And just as before, Mason flashed in front of her. When she spun around again, he stood behind her. His free paw hovered over a bump on his chest. It was a device of some kind, like a remote control. It had been stuffed under his fur so he could activate it with a simple tap of a button.

She made a move to run again, but Mason held her in place, threatening to press the button again. By then, the other bears had caught up. One bear ripped the tablet from her paws while another shoved her from behind, sending her to her knees. She immediately regretted not smashing the tablet on a tombstone.

Like a good bear, a well-trained warrior, Spark searched for an escape route. Or a weak spot among the bears, someone she could overpower. But there was nowhere to go. Even if she could break free, Mason would block her path again. Furious, she gripped a hunk of grass and tore it from the dirt. They tricked her. And now they had defeated her.

TWENTY-THREE

The bears closed in around her.

"How did you figure it out?" Mason asked.

There was no use lying. Besides, maybe she could stall them with the truth. "You have Loretta's knife," Spark said. "That means you were snooping around in the abandoned hospital wing after the children left. You're hiding something there. And then you didn't destroy the portal like you said you would."

Mason nodded his head grudgingly.

"You have some kind of scratcher under your fur," Spark said. "That's why you're so fast."

"I will have you know that I am quite fast without it. But yes, it is a scratcher. A prototype. I based its design on the scratcher that Jakmal stole from us. But it only works in this world—it cannot get you to another. Not yet."

"You're not trying to close the portal," Spark said. "Why?"

Two bears stood on either side of her. They gripped her arms and forced her to stand.

"What have you done with the Grand Sleuth?" she asked.

Everyone turned to Agnes. "Spark, we *are* the Grand Sleuth," she said. "What's left of it. We are the only ones standing between this world and the apocalypse."

"What do you mean? Why are you messing with the portals?"

"My child," she said, "there is so much to explain."

"Then answer me!" Spark said.

"We are trying to build a new scratcher. We have no other choice."

"You don't know what you're doing!" Spark said, scanning the crowd for anyone who would listen. "The portals are unstable. You said so yourself. They can swallow an entire city if they get too big. They could—"

"We know the risks," Agnes said.

"We do not have to tell her anything," Mason said. He stood before Spark, sneering at her. "I told you this bear was trouble. We have come too far to let her interfere. She's only got a few weeks left anyway. A few months at best."

"Until what?" Spark said.

"Until the final light!"

He said it to hurt her. And it worked. The words hit her like a fist in the jaw.

"That is enough," Agnes said. "This bear is one of us. She has proven herself. So she deserves to know the truth."

The guard bears relaxed, though their paws still held Spark secure.

"The League has always been at war with the monsters," Agnes said. "But the Grand Sleuth is working toward peace."

"Peace!" Spark shouted. "Peace? The monsters steal children! What're you gonna do? Talk to their lawyers?"

Agnes stepped closer. "I understand your anger. I really do."

"So how does your peace work?" Spark said. "What do the bears get out of it?"

"We have to open another portal," Agnes said. "That's why we need to study this one, to learn how. After that, the war will be over."

"*After* that?"

"Spark, please—"

"But what happens *during*?"

"Spark. This is the only way we can prevail. If we do not make this sacrifice, the price that comes later will be unbearable."

"Sacrifice," Spark hissed.

She could see the determination in the other bears' eyes. Each of them must have had doubts when they first heard this plan. And yet Agnes had convinced them all.

"We still want you to join us," Agnes said. "Your destiny is with the Grand Sleuth."

Spark sagged, and the two guards held her upright. She shook her head and laughed at her predicament.

"Do you agree with that, Mason?" Spark asked. "Have I passed enough of your tests?"

Mason eyed her. "You are a brave bear," he said. It was the best he could manage.

"What about the knife? I must have hit the target. You didn't think I could, did you?"

A few of the bears laughed.

Mason smiled and patted the blade on his paw. "As a matter of fact, you—"

With her arms still restrained, Spark jumped up and kicked Mason right in the button on his chest. He vanished, and the knife hung in the air for a split second before dropping to the ground. Somewhere behind her, he reappeared in midair and fell into the crowd. Before her captors could react, Spark wrenched her paws free and grabbed the handle of the knife. Swinging wildly, she forced her captors to back away. The bear to her right was too slow, and the blade sliced open his fur. A clump of white stuffing bloomed from the cut. The bear clamped the wound and dropped to his knees.

Spark dashed frantically through the tombstones while the bears gave chase. Like wolves tracking a lone rabbit, some of them followed her while others tried to cut off her escape. She knew she would not reach the exit before Mason teleported to her location. There was only one way out—a way that even the Grand Sleuth dared not follow.

Spark pocketed the knife as she neared the base of the tree. While she climbed, the bears swarmed around her. Someone grabbed her boot but she kicked it away, leaving her foot bare. Another paw snagged her belt. She unhooked it and the entire contraption fell away, including her sword, which clattered against the bark.

The bird's nest hung over her, creating a dark void. She scrambled up the trunk and reached into the portal. As she pulled herself inside, the gravity shifted. Her stomach lurched as she suddenly found herself on the cobblestone floor again, facedown, halfway through the doorframe. She got to her feet and slammed the door shut. The sound echoed through the hall before dying out like a distant thunderstorm.

She leaned against the wood and slid to the floor. The torches flickered softly. For a few seconds, it almost felt like home.

Before she could get too comfortable, she heard the voice of Agnes in her imagination:

My child.

My little cub.

You think you're safe here?

TWENTY-FOUR

The crack on the hallway ceiling had grown larger. A chunk of ancient mortar broke free and clattered to the floor in a cloud of dust. The fortress was crumbling under some enormous pressure. It had to be the volcano, Spark thought. She needed to get out.

Spark tried the first door she came across. It was locked. The second and third would not budge either. After the fourth one, she returned to the door through which she had come, only to find it locked as well. Had the bears on the other side destroyed the portal already? Or had it locked behind her automatically?

The last time she was trapped in Jakmal's castle, Spark found her way back by calling Loretta's name. When she called out this time, no one answered. The echo died in the hall.

"Stupid," she said as she slumped against the wall.

Was it all a lie? Including the vision that Agnes had shown her inside Molly's mind? No, if nothing else, *that* was real. Whatever Agnes planned to do, she thought it would protect Molly. At all costs, it seemed. But that left Loretta and Matthew vulnerable. All monsters worked this way—they separated people from their allies, then attacked them at their weakest moments. Whether it was a bully at school or a twisted creature from your nightmares, it worked the same every time. Split the juro, then strike.

Just like the doors, the drawbridge was locked as well. Spark tried to operate the lever that would lower it over the moat, but it wouldn't move an inch. She turned back to face the endless hallway. There was an infinite number of doors to try. One of them had to lead *somewhere*.

With so many of the torches out, Spark needed to pass through pockets of darkness to make her way through the hall. Each time, she scurried like a rat. More than once, she slipped on a loose stone, and a panic seized her as she righted herself and kept running.

All of the doors were locked. Before long, the drawbridge was so far away that the hall appeared to go on forever in both directions. She could no longer tell which way she had come. Forward and backward looked the same. She wondered if perhaps there was a portal in the middle of the hall, so that intruders would keep walking through on an endless loop without even realizing.

She ventured deeper and deeper into the castle, with no end in sight, until at last she saw something different. In the distance, a large dark shape blocked her way. As she got closer, she saw that a boulder had burst through the ceiling, leaving behind a massive hole. An orange glow penetrated the darkness, casting light on the rubble. The boulder must have rolled from the side of the mountain and plummeted from a great height.

Spark climbed the pile of rubble to the hole in the ceiling. She emerged at the base of the castle keep—a boxy tower built directly into the mountain. Spark turned in a full circle, amazed. It was impossible for her to be standing here. She must have traveled nearly a mile into the hall, yet the keep stood no more than twenty yards behind the main drawbridge. The magic of this place made it possible.

The landscape around the castle was a desolate expanse of rocks veined with glowing rivers of lava. Scorch marks blackened the walls of the keep. Boulders littered the castle grounds, leaving dents and craters everywhere. The truth finally began to hit Spark. This was no eruption, nor an earthquake. The castle had been attacked. But who would dare? And where was Jakmal?

Some of the boulders, she suddenly realized, were not boulders at all. Spark approached one and found it to be a strange creature. An arrow had pierced its side. Spark poked it. The monster was dead. Its body was thin and leathery. Claws sprouted from all four of its limbs. Its skeletal face had a mouth that opened sideways and brimmed with needle-like teeth. It had four red eyes, like a spider.

These were manglers—the same creatures that Jakmal fought before the curse transformed him into a monster himself. Spark recognized them from Sir Reginald's descriptions. From the looks of it, an entire mangler army had attacked the castle. They had slammed into the drawbridge, the only part of the castle not made of stone. But the drawbridge held. Barely. This mangler had made it over the wall before being taken down. They must have wanted Jakmal's castle full of portals. What monster wouldn't?

Spark hoped she would find more answers at the top of the keep. Leaving the hole in the roof behind, she began to climb. The once smooth surface had been badly dented in the attack, providing pawholds as she worked her way up.

Spark reached the parapet, the low wall at the top of the keep. When she pulled herself over the edge, she froze, her throat releasing a tiny gasp. There, on the other side of the wooden platform, stood Jakmal, his massive form dwarfing hers, his forked tail slithering about. He leaned on the wall with his back to her, his shoulders heaving with each breath. An enormous wooden crossbow lay at his feet next to a pile of arrows. No human could ever lift it, but Jakmal had used it to fight off an army of the worst monsters imaginable. Worse even than him.

But no, that wasn't right. His name was not Jakmal. That was merely a name given to him by the ones he frightened. She was looking at Jak. His brother, Mal, was fused to his body, the result of the curse that had transformed these imaginary friends into a single creature. Seeing them up close, Spark remembered that they were two people, not one. Jak and Mal. It was so hard to keep it all straight in her head.

Spark remained still, ready to leap off the tower if the monster spotted her. From behind, Jak's unnatural shape looked even more grotesque. His thin insect-like legs sprouted from the sides of his scorpion body. At his waist, his scales gave way to the pale skin of his torso, covered partially by a coat of chain-mail armor. The horns on his forehead curled over his skull. The pincer at the end of his tail gripped a steel arrow, ready to reload his crossbow at the first sign of trouble.

A huge gash in his chain mail exposed a deep cut in his arm, just above the elbow, still bleeding. When he shifted to the side, Spark saw the necklace on his chest that still gave her nightmares. The medallion encased the shriveled face of Mal. With their cursed bodies merged together into this abomination, they could feel each other's pain. Though Mal's eyes were open, his lids quivered with fatigue, and the dehydrated mouth smacked its lips. His skin had lost all color.

There was no mistaking it. Mal was dying.

Spark was so horrified by this scene that she neglected to duck behind the parapet when Mal's eyes suddenly opened wide and fixed on her. And once Mal saw her, Jak did, too. His pincer lifted over his head, making him look even taller and more menacing.

Before he could lunge at her, a terrible screech sounded from the other side of the keep. It was like a tire squealing and glass shattering all at once. Behind Jak, a mangler crawled on top of the parapet, its four legs crouched into fighting position.

Spark pointed to the monster. Jak turned too late. The creature sprang from the wall and latched onto his back. The monsters tumbled along the ground, splintering the wood. The mangler wrapped its claws around Jak's neck while pinning his tail with its hind legs. Jak tried to break free, but the mangler's nails dug into his skin, refusing to let go.

Mal looked at Spark, begging for help—until one of the mangler's hands clamped down on his face.

Spark couldn't help doing what she did next. She leapt from the parapet and landed beside the two monsters.

"Hey!" she shouted.

The mangler yelped and tore itself away from Jak. There was nothing monsters feared more than a teddy bear.

Spark spoke the same words that all bears used when faced with a monster. "I am Spark. I am the sworn protector of this . . . house." She winced at how ridiculous that sounded, but the monster didn't seem to notice. "We serve goodness and truth," she continued. "We give refuge to the innocent. We defend the light, to the final light, in times of darkness."

The mangler scrambled away, cowering against the wall. *Good, yes, be afraid*, Spark thought. *You're not so tough without your friends.*

"By the power bestowed upon me by the League of Ursus, I command you to be gone!"

The mangler pointed at her with a claw and groaned, its hinged mouth opening sideways. Even without words, Spark knew what this meant. The mangler wanted her to know that they would meet again. And the next time, there would be more of them.

Then it jumped over the parapet and vanished.

Slowly, Jak got to his feet. His tail hung limp, and his two enormous hands cradled Mal's face. The wound on his arm was still bleeding. Both of the faces grimaced in unison.

"I'm not your enemy," Spark said. "I helped you because I need you to help me. And if you don't, we're both in big trouble."

Jak stared at her, seemingly offended that this little toy would dare lecture him in his own castle. He gestured to the cut on his arm. She understood: whatever they needed to do would have to wait until Jak could patch up his wounds. With that, the monster dragged his tail across the floor and descended the steps into the castle keep.

Far away, one of the wounded manglers groaned as it retreated with the others.

"Okay, did that just happen?" Spark said aloud. *Yeah*, she thought. *It really did.*

She walked over to the staircase and followed the monster into the heart of the castle.

TWENTY-FIVE

As Spark descended into the depths of the tower, the sorcery of the place once again played tricks on her. The staircase twisted far below into what should have been the molten rock beneath the volcano's crust. Yet this area felt as cold as any other in the castle. When she looked up, the hole in the ceiling was a mere a dot, the torches on the walls forming a galaxy around it. She would find nothing by returning the way she came. She had no choice but to keep going down.

Several times, she peeked over the railing to see the bottom, only to find that the staircase kept going. She grew dizzy from the constant spiraling. Growing impatient, she ran at full speed until she slipped on a loose stone and tumbled down the stairs. At last she struck a flat surface and rolled to a halt. And like that, she had reached the lowest level, a bare chamber with an arched doorway ringed with diamond-shaped stones.

She recognized the grunt coming from inside the archway. If Jak meant it as a warning, he didn't put much effort into it. He was the only one who could get her back home. Now that she knew the Grand Sleuth was making deals with monsters, making a deal with him didn't seem so crazy.

Spark entered the chamber. To her surprise, it looked like a child's room, complete with a tiny bed and a writing desk. On the desk, a tarp covered a large square object with a set of tools piled in front. It looked like some kind of science project. A pair of red velvet curtains framed a window, though the opening was sealed over with bricks. A few paintings hung on the walls. Some of them featured gallant knights in armor riding on horseback, while others showed bearded men in fancy ruffled outfits from hundreds of years ago. A rug made of an animal's fur lay on the floor in front of a charred fireplace.

Jak and Mal had once been the imaginary friends of a child, the son of a village elder. Was this a copy of that child's bedroom? Was this where they truly felt safe and at home?

Jak was crouched in a corner, his tail curled protectively around his body. Beside him, a set of primitive medical instruments was splayed on top of a small table. Jak gritted his fangs as he attempted to stitch the wound on his arm, while Mal's face twisted in agony. It was no use. Furious, Jak tossed the table across the room, where it collapsed and splintered against the wall only a few feet from Spark.

Jak cradled his brother's exhausted face. The two monsters wept without making a sound, a silence that conveyed their regret and anger over what they had become. Knowing that Spark stood nearby, Jak faced the wall so she would not see the worst of it. This enormous monster blubbering like a child.

Spark remembered the time she'd stitched Sir Reginald back together. "I can help," she said.

Her offer only made Jak and Mal cry harder.

"I've done this before," she said. "I'm not here to fight you. I know who you really are." She plucked a needle and thread from among the instruments scattered on the floor. "Let me try."

The monster slowly uncoiled his tail. When Spark first met Jak, in Loretta's bedroom, he had made a point of standing as tall as he could in order to frighten her. Now he crouched before her, awaiting orders.

"I need that torch," Spark said, pointing to the one next to him. Jak pulled it from its cradle. "Hold it out," she added. "I need the flame."

She waved the needle over the fire until it became red-hot. This would kill any germs. Sewing a bear together was easy, but flesh required some precautions. She nodded to indicate that the needle was ready. While Jak returned the torch to its cradle, the face on his chest saw Spark approaching. Mal's eyes and mouth opened wide. Jak soothed his brother by placing his hands on Mal's forehead and whispering something in a language Spark did not understand. The face grew calmer, but the eyes slammed shut.

Spark examined the cut on Jak's bicep. She could not tell how deep it went. If Jak was letting her do this, then he expected it to work. Monster biology would have to do the rest.

She began at the bottom of the wound. With one hand on Mal's forehead, Jak used his other hand to grip the velvet curtain. As the needle penetrated the skin, both faces scrunched in exactly the same way, with their brows knitted and jaws clenched. On the second stitch, Jak's tail lashed. On the third, he tore the curtain free.

"Almost done," Spark said.

While Spark sutured the wound, she stole a glance at the object under the tarp. From this angle, she could see a black metal tube sticking out. It was the business end of a scratcher, the machine that could create a portal to her world. Spark had destroyed it in her last encounter with Jakmal—or so she thought. Now it looked like Jak was trying to fix it. If he succeeded, the machine could get her home. But perhaps her sacred duty called on her to sacrifice herself and smash it for good. It was a grim thought.

Jak shifted, and Spark refocused on the task at hand. After the fifth stitch, he growled at her.

"I have to finish!"

Spark went for another loop. Jak shoved her away.

"Tell me about your friend," she said.

Jak stared at her.

"Your friend. The little boy."

Jak pointed above the fireplace. On the mantel were two figurines, a few inches tall, carved from soapstone. They depicted a pair of knights, both with horned helmets, holding their swords at the hilt so the blades rested at their feet.

"That's you and your brother, right?"

Jak nodded.

Spark got ready for the next stitch. Jak did not resist this time.

"Did your friend make those?" Spark asked.

Jak nodded.

"He's pretty good!" Spark said. "Wait. Which came first—the figurines or you?"

Jak slapped his palm on his chest, barely missing Mal's face. He gave her a look that said, *What are you, ignorant?*

"Okay, I got it. You came first."

She pulled another stitch through. Jak's arm remained still.

"He played games with you guys, huh? Came up with little adventures for you."

Jak's mouth did something that could have been a smile, though it was hard to tell through his fangs.

"Kinda like Loretta. Maybe if she were around back then, she'd make up stories with little carved statues instead of with movies."

Finally, Spark broke off the end of the thread and tied it into a tight little knot. Jak gingerly tapped the wound with his fingers. He retreated to the corner.

"You have to keep it clean and dry," Spark said.

She remembered the time Loretta needed stitches after accidentally cutting her arm on a broken pane of glass. By day six, the sutures began to itch like crazy, and Loretta begged to get them taken out. Spark expected Jak to show the same amount of patience.

"Hey," she said as he curled into a protective ball. "Hey, um, I need to get out of here."

Jak began to hum a tune, a lullaby of some kind.

"Can you understand me?" Spark asked.

Mal joined the humming, though his voice was weak and raspy.

"Hel-*lo*," Spark said.

Nothing. The monster was in his own world, a happy place inside his mind.

"You're just like my sock monkey friend," she said with a sigh.

Spark decided to leave him there. If he wasn't going to help, she needed to find a portal on her own. She exited the fake child's room and went to the great spiral staircase that twisted endlessly into the darkness. The lullaby echoed through the stairwell, so soft and sweet that Spark could hardly believe it came from something as terrible as a monster.

TWENTY-SIX

Spark leaned on the parapet. The volcano churned behind her, rivulets of lava reaching like golden fingers around the castle. Scorched, cracked earth stretched out endlessly beneath a sky permanently darkened with ash. If Matthew had written this scene into one of his scripts, Loretta would have asked him to cut it. "It's too much," she would have said. "We're already sad. You don't have to beat us over the head with it."

Spark was losing nearly all hope of getting out. Jak must have shut down all the portals during the attack. She couldn't blame him for that, but she couldn't reason with him either, not from what she had just seen.

Maybe the power that Agnes had shown her could work now. *Think of Loretta*, Agnes had said. *Think of all you hold dear*. Sure, Spark could do that. She had done little else these past few weeks.

Agnes had also said to let Loretta do the work. *The child possesses the power, not the bear*. So Spark tried to think of Loretta working at her desk, typing out new stories or commenting on Matthew's storyboards. Occasionally crumpling the paper into a ball and slam-dunking it in the trash bin—a failure turned into the jubilant act of starting over. Spark's concentration faded when she imagined flaunting this sacred power in front of Agnes. The look on the pink bear's face would be priceless! But this soon became too distracting; Spark was losing focus. "Come on, think," she said. But every time she tried, Agnes would waddle into her vision to scold her for not getting it right.

Something scraped along the floor behind her. Spark spun around so fast she almost fell off the parapet. Jak was approaching, his tail dragging behind him. He stared at her for a few seconds. The stitches on his arm still held, though the skin around it was red and inflamed.

"Are you ready to talk now?" she asked.

He waved his hand in a "Follow me" gesture.

"No, I've had it with your creepy castle. Can't you just—"

He waved more forcefully this time. A fang poked out from his curled lip.

"Well, when you put it that way," Spark grumbled.

She followed as Jak limped to the stairwell. She kept her distance, however, as the pincer at the end of his tail opened and closed of its own accord. They began the long walk down the spiral stairs.

Spark decided to try one more time. "If you help me get out of here, I swear I'll find a way to lift your curse," she said. "I know you think Loretta can help you, but maybe I can too. There have to be some good bears in the Grand Sleuth. Maybe we can—"

To her stunned surprise, they reached the bottom level after descending a mere two stories. It made no sense. Spark dropped to her knees and patted the floor while gazing at the top of the staircase. It was the magic again. She would never understand it.

They passed through an arched doorway into a circular room with an enormous domed ceiling, painted dark blue and pocked with stars. It was a map of the heavens and the major constellations. In the center of the room, two globes stood side by side.

The green-and-blue one represented Earth. Spark figured that the black-and-orange one represented this barren world, a planet with no name.

A series of murals extended all the way around the room. They were frescoes, images painted onto a wall of wet plaster. On the floor in front of each scene, an oil lamp illuminated the paintings, making them appear taller and more menacing. Cracks in the wall cast sinister shadows onto the ceiling.

The first painting depicted a storm cloud brewing above a mountaintop, with a village nestled in the valley below. As Spark drew closer, the cloud broke apart into little pieces. She blinked, assuming that her eyes needed to adjust to the light. But the movement continued as the painting came to life. The cloud became a horde of manglers descending upon the town, their bodies cascading into the valley like an avalanche. As soon as Spark stepped away, the fresco returned to its original form—just an artist's rendition of some rainy weather over a quiet village.

Jak nudged her toward the next painting, which showed a troop of bears battling the monsters. Spark held in a giggle when she noticed that the painter depicted the teddy bears as massive beasts, much larger than grizzlies and wearing elaborate armor and helmets. With their swords and spears, they hacked their way through the monsters. The scene moved as the lead bear slashed her blade, the manglers hissing and spitting at her.

"The general," Spark said. The bear in the painting was the leader of the very first juro—the squad of bears who swore an oath of loyalty to one another. Together, they formed the League of Ursus and became its high council.

In the third painting, two knights stood triumphant over the bodies of the manglers. This was Jak and Mal when they were still a little boy's heroic imaginary friends. Their golden armor gleamed so bright that Spark needed to shield her eyes. Behind them, the remnants of the monster horde retreated, resembling ash rising high above a bonfire.

Spark knew what she would find in the next painting. Jak knelt before his injured brother while the wizard bear—the hexen—pointed his staff at them. The general waited in the distance, either not seeing or not wanting to see what the hexen was doing. The image moved as the two brothers fused into a hideous new form. A tail sprouted from their conjoined body as their faces twisted with rage.

The painting that followed seemed completely out of place. In it, a young boy wrapped in a blanket stared out a window, holding a candle in his hand while raindrops pelted the glass. His tightened face suggested that he held back tears. Spark recognized the curtains, and the fireplace, and the desk with two wooden figurines on top. This was the child who had conjured Jak and Mal from his mind and gave them life. Spark waited for the image to move like the others, but it remained still. The boy would stay sad forever, it seemed, wondering what had happened to the two golden knights who used to protect him.

After that, the frescoes depicted other children with the same pathetic expression, each cowering in their rooms, hiding behind desks or under beds or in closets. And in every one, the child's teddy bear waited nearby, either propped on a pillow or sitting in a chair or resting on a shelf. If a human were to view these paintings, they wouldn't notice anything out of the ordinary. To Spark, however, it appeared that the bears sat by and did nothing while their dusas hid in fear.

"What is this?" Spark asked. "What am I looking at?"

Jak merely pointed at the image, as if the message were obvious.

The next fresco was almost entirely black, save for a square of light in the center. Half in shadow, three faces stared rapturously at the source of the light. Two girls and a boy. Spark needed to step back a bit to realize that they were in a modern movie theater, their gaze fixed on a screen.

"Loretta?" Spark said. Despite her tiny size, Spark squared her shoulders toward Jak. "You wanna threaten me? Is that it?"

Jak grunted in annoyance and pointed to the corner of the painting. This image moved as well, though with a subtle change. A pair of eyes appeared and disappeared in the background. She recognized them. They belonged to the smiling man. Spark hurried to the end of the frescoes, only to find that the last few were incomplete, and the final section of the wall was blank. Spark could only guess that these paintings showed things that would happen in the future. They were not set in stone just yet.

In the first of these unfinished paintings, Jak appeared in the center, with Loretta, Matthew, and Sofia forming a circle around him. Spark could not tell if the monster held the children prisoner or if they were—

—if they were helping him. They were *curing* him and his brother, she realized.

"So . . . you weren't expecting to steal Loretta's power, whatever it might be," Spark said. "You were expecting her to heal you. By her own choice."

Jak nodded.

"I can't say I approve of your methods," Spark grumbled.

In the next one, a great army gathered on a barren, rocky landscape. The soldiers were all monsters, marching behind the slim figure of the smiling man.

"And this smiley-face guy is after her. And the Grand Sleuth is letting him do it. But why?"

Jak pointed at the image, urging her to look closer. When she did, she saw a tiny figure walking slightly behind the smiling man. Barely a smudge of paint, a girl with dark hair. It was Loretta. And even worse: she was terrified.

Spark turned to the next fresco, hoping it would show her what would happen. But it remained blank, mocking her. Nothing but a gray stillness, like a heavy fog.

And when she stepped back, Spark noticed something terrible. The future in which Loretta would heal Jakmal was slowly fading from the wall. It became blurrier, cloudier. Next to it, the other future, the one with the monster army, began to fill in details. More creatures joined. The landscape became clearer. Loretta's face became more distinct. Paler. Sadder.

Spark had her answer. And the weight of it forced her to sit down and stare at the two paintings.

Behind her, Jak's tail scraped along the floor as he headed for the staircase. As she sat there, she listened to his footsteps ascending the tower. He left her to her jumbled thoughts.

TWENTY-SEVEN

Spark paced around the map room for a while. Without Jak there to enchant them, the images had stilled again, the paint cracked and flaking. She lifted one of the oil lamps and held it closer to the frescoes, but nothing moved. This magic place was suddenly stale and old, just like the cobwebbed mausoleum.

Holding the lamp by its wire handle, she passed each of the images of the children. The boy under the bed. The girl in the closet. Spark lingered on the children in the theater. She wanted to jump into the painting, to warn them about the evil that lurked in the dark. Somehow, Jak captured their expressions perfectly. As the only official teenager in the group, Sofia smirked at the screen, pretending to be unimpressed. Loretta gazed at it in wonder, a smile spreading across her face. Matthew leaned forward, his features serious, taking in every frame and filing it away.

Spark continued along until one of the frescoes made her stop and hold the lamp closer. A frail girl in a nightgown sat at a miniature kitchen table. She pretended to sip tea from a plastic cup. A pink teddy bear sat in a smaller chair beside her, an empty cup in her saucer.

Spark placed her paw on the girl's cheek. "Molly," she whispered.

"You saw it all coming. And your own bear wouldn't listen."

Something buzzed in the pocket of her army jacket. Spark remembered that she still had the burner phone Mason had given her. She flipped it open and pressed it to her ear.

"Hello?"

"Spark. Are you all right?"

It was Agnes.

"How are you reaching me?" Spark asked.

"Mason was able to modify the phone, thanks to the data we collected from the portal. Besides, even though you're in another world, you're not that far away in physical space."

"Congratulations. Glad I could help."

"I wanted to talk some sense into you, in case you're planning something foolish."

"Oh, I'm honored," Spark said, channeling Loretta's most sarcastic tone.

"I take it the mangler attack has failed."

"You knew about that. They were after the scratcher, weren't they? Did the smiling man send them?"

"I tried to stop you from going there, Spark. Remember?"

"But you knew. Because you signed a peace treaty with the enemy."

"A treaty that *you* have put in jeopardy. And now no one is safe."

"Peace won't make you safe. And it can't be worth all this trouble."

"You think that way because you protect one dusa. We protect *all* of them."

"And how will you do that?"

"By preventing what happened last time!" Agnes snapped. She had never raised her voice before. "I was there when the monsters formed an army against us. A long time ago, before you were even

151

made. We stopped them in the end. But the price was so high. I vowed to find another way."

"Your other way is called surrender."

"It is called survival. It will prevent future attacks. And it will save lives."

"You still haven't told me how. What's your big plan?"

Agnes paused. Spark imagined the other bears gathered around her in the playroom at the hospital, listening in.

"The bald man with the big smile," Agnes began. "He has a name. They call him Karacor."

Spark had never heard this name before. But it didn't sound good.

Agnes continued. "He was the one who raised an army of monsters. We defeated him. Barely. And ever since then, he's been a pest. A plunderer. He finds portals into our world, feeds off the fear of children, and then heads back to his."

"So what?" Spark said. "That's what monsters do."

"After Jakmal stole the scratcher from us, he created new portals everywhere. Karacor found one and came here, along with some other monsters."

"But then I destroyed the scratcher."

"Yes. And it had a ripple effect. Most of the portals closed. The monsters were stranded here."

"How many?"

"More than we can handle," Agnes said. "But that's not the biggest problem. After we defeated him the last time, Karacor was completely disgraced. Even the other monsters wanted nothing to do with him. But when they found themselves trapped here they were desperate for a leader, and he came along at just the right time. This is his chance to take back what we took from him. And now they have us surrounded."

"They're planning to attack the hospital."

"They're *at* the hospital," Agnes said. "They're everywhere. They would have wiped us out if we hadn't offered them a deal."

"So you agreed to open a portal for them," Spark said. "So they can get back to their world. And so you can save your yourselves. But why can't they go back through the portal I found?"

"There are many monster worlds," Agnes said. "Jakmal's is only one of them."

Spark took a moment to marvel at this revelation. Then she continued putting the pieces together.

"I get it now," Spark said. "You made a promise you couldn't keep. They thought you had a scratcher, but it was gone."

"You left us with no choice," Agnes said. "Our only option was to build another one."

"From scratch?"

Agnes paused. "That isn't funny."

"You used me to find that portal because you needed it to complete your work," Spark said. "Mason was studying it so he could finish his scratcher."

"That's right. We debated for days whether to tell you the truth. But it had to be this way. There is too much at stake."

"So, you give Karacor what he wants. What do we get in return?"

"We get to keep the scratcher, use it to close all the portals for good. Then we rebuild the League. Restore order."

"He's just gonna let us do that," Spark said, shaking her head.

"Yes. Karacor wants to leave so he can rule his own world. He has scores to settle with the other monsters. When we open the portal, he will rejoin his minions on the other side, and we will never see him again."

"But his minions tried to take Jak's castle. That castle has portals that lead to many worlds, including ours."

"We have to deal with the problems in front of us," Agnes said.

"If all goes as planned, this will end the war. It's been the dream of every Grand Sleuth and we can finally make it happen. Or we can keep fighting forever. Until one day, some monster becomes powerful enough to open a portal so big it can never be closed. If that ever happens, there will be no difference between our world and theirs. No boundary between the two. Is that what you want?"

Spark remembered the portal that Jak had created in the attic of Loretta's house, how it expanded outward, threatening to engulf the entire house. What Agnes had in mind sounded infinitely worse.

"Well, looks like you got this all figured out," Spark said. "Except for the most important thing."

"And that is?"

"Karacor has one more demand. He wants to take Loretta with him to this other world. Jak showed me."

Agnes was silent.

"Did you hear me?" Spark shouted. "I said your monster friend wants to steal my dusa! She can create portals—*without a scratcher*—and I'll bet you anything Karacor knows that! That's why he was lurking outside our house! He's going to take her away. Even if you close every last portal, it won't matter. He'll use her power to return."

The phone went silent for a long time.

"Hello?" Spark said.

"I'm sorry," Agnes said. "We've come too far. There's too much at stake. We must see this through to the end."

Spark felt as though someone had splashed cold water in her face. "You would betray everything we stand for to save your own skins?"

"Whether you realize it or not, I've been trying to save yours as well."

"Me?"

"Mason is right. You have so little time left. Soon your dusa will grow up and move on. But if you join us, your story will not end. You will pass from one dusa to the next, as I have. Your name will change, many times in fact. But your mission will remain."

Spark had been too distracted by her mission to think about the final light. But Agnes's suggestion felt like a dam bursting, flooding her with all the doubts and fears she had hidden away.

"I have heard that the final light can happen at any instant," Agnes said. "In the middle of a sentence you're speaking, or a thought you're having. That would be so unfair, after all you have done. Think of all the good you could do with just a little more time."

No, Spark thought. There had to be another way. Wait, that wasn't right: there didn't have to be another way. But maybe she could make one. She could carve it out somehow. Anything to avoid surrender. Anything to protect Loretta.

"How close are you to finishing your scratcher?" Spark asked. "I mean, I guess it all depends on that, doesn't it?"

"Very close."

Spark felt herself tumbling off a cliff as the next words spilled out of her.

"You just made a big mistake," Spark said.

"Did I?"

"Now I know what I'm after. I'm coming to destroy your scratcher. You better stay out of my way."

"I can't let you do that."

"You would do the same thing for Molly."

"I'm doing *all* of this for Molly," Agnes said. She sounded so defeated. Spark understood now. All the treaties and wars meant nothing compared to the love that a bear felt for her dusa. Karacor knew this. He knew how to get a bear to do his bidding.

"You can expect another visit from the manglers," Agnes said.

"I'll be ready."

"A shame," Agnes whispered. "I had so much to teach you."

Spark turned to the painting of Molly's tea party. Agnes looked so innocent and happy, almost like another child.

"Good luck to you, little cub," Agnes said.

Spark threw the cellphone at the wall, where it shattered against the pink bear's face.

Then she plopped onto the ground and curled her stubby legs into her chest. It would be morning soon on the other side. She needed to go home.

TWENTY-EIGHT

"Come on, let me help!" Spark said.

She waited atop the castle keep while Jak screwed a metal plate onto the side of the scratcher. The device rested on a wooden stool so that it could be aimed over the parapet. The first time she saw it, Spark thought the scratcher resembled a film projector: a rectangular steel box with a tube sticking out of the front. At the end of the tube, a crystal acted as a lens, beaming the portal out through a combination of science and magic.

Up close, however, Spark could see that the machine was in bad shape, dented and scratched and missing several buttons. Needle gauges twitched and dull lights blinked, and Spark couldn't tell if they were merely broken or if they indicated some kind of danger. The only high-tech element was a digital panel, which displayed a set of random numbers. Spark assumed these were the coordinates for other worlds.

When Jak finished sealing the metal plate, he dropped the screwdriver on the floor. Next, he moved on to the crystal, which he plucked from the tube and examined with a magnifying glass. Spark noticed a random screw jutting out from the bottom of the scratcher. Assuming that Jak had missed it, she took the screwdriver and tried to tighten it. The monster shooed her away with a grunt.

"Okay, fine!" she said.

When Jak turned away, she tried again. But before she could move it a centimeter, she felt herself lifted from the floor, carried to the wall, and dropped there. Jak shoved his palm in her face—a clear message to stay away.

"How long is this gonna take?" Spark grumbled.

As the monster turned around, the pincer on the end of his tail snatched the screwdriver from her paws.

While Jak worked, the face on his chest appeared to be asleep. The skin around the stitches still looked red and irritated. The manglers may have held poison in their claws. That would explain why Jak sometimes pressed his palm against the wound, his face twisting in pain.

"I'm sorry," Spark said.

Jak glanced at her, then continued his work.

"I just realized that no one ever said sorry for what the League did to you," she said. She supposed that, as a member of the League, she owed him an apology as much as any bear. Jak positioned himself so that he wouldn't have to look at her.

"Is it too late?" she asked.

Maybe it was. No one really knew how long Jak and Mal had lived like this, or what they went through to get here.

"Loretta has a friend named Darcy," Spark said. "They didn't like each other at first. You know why?"

Jak ignored her.

"It was because Loretta brought me to school one day for show and tell, and Darcy grabbed me and bit my ear. She thought I would taste like chocolate! Loretta was so mad she stayed in a corner for the rest of the day. But then Darcy, Claire, and Jisha gathered some flowers outside and brought them to Loretta. Darcy apologized, and

Loretta forgave her. They've all been friends ever since. And they still like to tell that story."

Spark decided not to mention that it was Darcy's polar bear Ozzie who had slashed Jakmal with a circular saw, or that it was Jisha's panda Lulu who fired pellets at him with a slingshot.

"What if I said that I forgive you for stealing the children?" Spark asked. "Would that make a difference?"

Jak pressed a red button, and the scratcher hummed to life. The crystal glowed. He aimed it at the mountain. Spark had never witnessed the birth of a portal. As a beam of light extended from the machine to the rock face, she finally understood its awesome power. The ground shook. Boulders tumbled from the mountain, and another vein of lava burst from below the surface.

The beam formed a flat white circle on the mountainside. When Jak tweaked the controls, the circle puffed out into a three-dimensional sphere, a reflective bubble about five feet across. Jak turned the machine on its stool and the bubble followed his aim, floating away from the mountain. Spark saw her reflection sliding across the shiny surface. Jak guided the portal so that it hovered above the drawbridge, which was now open. That was how it worked. Out here, the portal could collapse. But if Jak could move it into the castle, the magical walls would keep the portal stable.

A red light flashed on the side of the scratcher, accompanied by an obnoxious buzzing. Jak fiddled with the controls again. Waves rippled across the portal, hardening into sharp spikes. Then the portal crumpled like a ball of tinfoil.

"What's happening?"

When Jak slammed the scratcher with his fist, Spark had her answer. The machine wasn't ready. It may never be ready.

The portal wobbled and shrank to the size of a basketball. Spark raced to the machine. "Can we restart it?" That always seemed to work with Loretta's computer.

Jak flicked a switch, and the red warning light turned off. Still the buzzing noise continued. Spark realized that the noise wasn't coming from the scratcher—it was coming from below. She spun around in a full circle to scan the area. It was too late. The manglers had returned. This was the noise they made when they traveled in packs.

A single claw reached over the parapet, its nails digging into the stone.

"Look out!" Spark cried.

The creature leapt onto Jak, pinning him to the ground. Then it let out a screech—a call to the others. More appeared, either crawling down from the mountain or climbing up the walls. Jak's pincered tail gripped the creature by the neck and ripped it off his back. More manglers tumbled over the parapet. They were supposed to be afraid of Spark. But in these numbers, they knew that a teddy bear could be defeated like anyone else.

Spark would not let things end like this. If she failed, she wanted it to be in her own world, facing Agnes and the Grand Sleuth. Before she could raise her stubby little fist, something plucked her from the floor. Jak took one last look at her before tossing her over the wall and toward the drawbridge. She somersaulted a few times before landing on the wood and skidding to a halt just before the moat.

Above her, the unstable portal pulsed and vibrated. Jak's message was clear: She should try to escape while she still could. Spark glanced up, but Jak and Mal were hidden behind the wall of the keep. It felt wrong to leave them like this. She had no choice.

As she reached for the portal, something heavy landed on the drawbridge, rattling the chains. A mangler stood between her and escape. She ran at the beast, screaming. Its claw swiped at her, but she flopped to her belly and slid between its legs. She scrambled to her feet again and jumped for the portal. Something grabbed at her as she entered it. Then everything went silent as she plummeted into darkness.

Spark remained still for a few seconds. Then she smelled something familiar: the scent of Loretta's shoes. She got to her feet and fumbled forward until she pushed open a door, flooding the closet with late afternoon sunlight. She was home again.

No one was around, so she crept across the floor to the shelf. Zed rose from his seated position, his wide mouth hanging open at the sight of her. She had never been happier to see him.

Instead of scrambling down the shelf to greet her, Zed propped himself on his hands, scrunched his face, and shot his tail straight into the air. His mouth became a perfect circle as he howled at her like a real monkey. "Oooh-oooh-oooh-ah-ah!"

"What?" she said, turning to the closet. "There's nothing there."

Something poked her shoulder. Spark realized too late that the mangler's hand had latched onto her.

"Gah! Get it off me! Get it off!"

The portal had closed so violently that it severed the monster's arm at the wrist. And yet the hand still lived. Its fingers crawled like a spider and wrapped around Spark's throat. She twirled, trying to free herself. Zed arrived, wielding a long paintbrush he'd swiped from Loretta's desk. While Spark wrestled with the claw, Zed tried to use the brush as a lever to pry the claw away. When that failed, he reared back and swung the brush like a sword. He missed.

"Ow!" Spark shouted.

She dropped to the floor and rolled around, but the claw squeezed tighter. Zed continued whacking at its fingers and knuckles.

"Open the bathroom door," she grunted. He stared at her, confused. "Do it!"

Zed disappeared into the hall. Spark followed him on all fours, the creature's nails poking through her fur. The bathroom door opened. She motioned for Zed to get onto the toilet tank. He finally understood what she was trying to do. He jumped on top and lifted the lid, slamming it against the tank. Spark climbed to the bowl and tried to pry the mangler's hand from her back.

"Get the plunger!" she said. "The plunger!"

Zed used the plunger as a spear, jabbing and prodding the hand until it finally fell off into the bowl. Now free, Spark reached for the handle and flushed. The water swirled around the hand as it desperately tried to swim. As the whirlpool dragged it into the pipe, its fingernails scraped the porcelain to slow its descent. Spark grabbed the plunger and drove it into the hand again and again while Zed flushed the toilet once more. At last, the claw vanished into the drain. A rattling shook the entire plumbing system as the water carried the evil away.

Spark allowed herself to fall from the toilet and land on the tiled floor.

Zed pulled anxiously at his little wool cap. "We got hands chasing us now? *Hands?!*"

He plopped down beside her. They enjoyed the coolness of the tiles for a few seconds.

Finally, Zed turned to her. "Are you okay?"

"Oh, I'm great, Zed. Thank you for asking. How are you?"

"Are there more . . . *hands* . . . where you came from?"

Spark considered this. With each passing second, Zed grew more tense, his tail flicking about. "There are a few," she finally said.

TWENTY-NINE

Finding herself home again should have made Spark feel relieved. Instead, it only made her realize how high the stakes had risen. Once they discovered that she had returned, the Grand Sleuth could take all of this away. And if they got their own scratcher working, no one would be safe.

Spark checked the clock radio in Loretta's room. Six in the evening, with the early spring sun dropping fast.

"Where is everyone?"

"They went to dinner at the Bombay," Zed said. Matthew's favorite restaurant. Typically, the family ate there when they wanted to celebrate. Spark wondered if the kids' grounding was finally over.

"Was the cemetery scary?" Zed asked, trembling a bit.

"My friend," Spark began, "the cemetery was the least scary part."

Zed's eyes widened. They grew wider still as she recounted the entire story, from finding the portal to the mangler army to her nail-biting escape.

Zed had a habit of fixating on a minor detail after listening to Spark's stories. This time was no exception.

"Did Jakmal accept your apology?" he asked. "I mean, Jak."

Spark paused. "I don't know. But he threw me into the portal. That must mean that he believes I can help him from this side."

"How?"

"I need to get the scratcher from the Grand Sleuth. After that, I don't know." Whether she kept it or destroyed it, Spark would have a huge target on her back. Which meant Loretta would be in danger, too. She would have to deal with that part later.

Outside, the family car pulled into the driveway. The doors clicked open.

Zed returned to his spot on the shelf. "Quick, tell me what I missed," Spark said.

"Oh, right! Mom and Dad agreed to let Loretta and Matthew go to the film festival. And the kids asked if they could bring their props to display in the exhibit hall."

"Wait, when is the festival again?"

The footsteps grew louder. Zed went limp. Spark realized that she was still in the middle of the floor, completely out of place, with Loretta on the way. With no time to climb to her spot on the shelf, she flopped onto her side and pretended to be any other inanimate object.

Loretta entered wearing her earbuds, which connected to the phone in her pocket. "You're still open, right?" she said. "Uh-huh. Uh-huh. Yeah."

She grabbed Zed and tucked him under her arm.

"I know, I'm so sorry," she said. The person on the other end sounded annoyed.

The sight of Spark out of place startled her. Luckily for Spark, the phone call distracted Loretta enough to make her think her bear simply fell off the shelf.

"I just had to work something out with my parents," Loretta said, picking up Spark and stuffing her next to Zed.

The person on the other end asked a question.

"I'm eleven," Loretta said. "Yes, I'm the one with the teddy bear movie."

Matthew appeared in the doorway. "Are we good?"

Loretta silenced him by pressing a finger to her lips. "Oh, that's so nice of you to say," she told the person on the phone. "Oh, thank you. Thanks." Loretta scrunched her nose in anticipation. The person said something she liked, and Loretta hopped up and down. "Oh my gosh, thank you so much. We'll be there right away."

Matthew pumped both fists like a Rock 'Em Sock 'Em Robot.

Loretta said goodbye and hung up the phone. Then she jumped in place a few more times, making Spark a little dizzy. "Okay, okay, it's not too late."

"You should be a lawyer!" Matthew said.

"Tell Dad we need to go right now."

Matthew headed for the stairs. "I'm on it!"

Loretta shoved Spark and Zed into a plastic shopping bag, which she then stuffed into her backpack. Everything went dark. The bag shook as Loretta ran to the car and dropped it on the seat. While Dad drove, Matthew fiddled with the radio from the passenger seat. Loretta barked orders from the rear.

"My app says take the highway," she said.

"I know how to get to the college," Dad said. "I don't need your appetizer."

Spark remembered that a local college hosted the film festival. She had lost track of time and forgotten that it started today.

When Dad's shortcut inevitably took too long, they playfully argued over whether he should've listened to Loretta. Spark liked the sound of the banter, their first friendly exchange in a week. Loretta decided to press her luck by asking about a forbidden topic.

"So, after we're done . . . you're okay dropping us off at Sofia's game, right?"

"What is this game again?" Dad said.

"It's the All-Star game. She's starting."

"Okay, but . . ." Dad scraped his stubbly beard. "If you see Mr. Lopez, don't bother him, all right? Don't apologize, don't wave hello, nothing. He's really mad. That goes especially for you, lover boy."

"Dad!" Matthew shouted.

The car pulled into a parking space. "Come on!" Loretta yelled, opening the door before it came to a complete stop.

"Slow down!" Dad said. "Do you even know where you're going?"

"Yes!"

With Matthew huffing and puffing beside her, Loretta ran maybe fifty yards before opening a door. By then, Spark and Zed had smushed together into a cramped knot of fur and cloth, trapped in a pocket of darkness that smelled like a peanut butter sandwich.

"Hi, we're here for the film festival," Loretta said to someone, maybe a security guard.

"Exhibit hall's that way."

"Thanks!"

After a few minutes of walking, they entered a large, echoey space where dozens of people milled about. Spark could hear hammers hitting nails and a forklift beeping as someone drove it in reverse.

"Hi, are you Nancy?" Loretta said.

"Yes."

"I'm Loretta! We talked on the phone a little bit ago."

"Oh, right! You made it just in time. We're about to close."

While Loretta thanked her, she pulled the plastic bag from her backpack. Spark tried to peek outside without rustling the plastic too much. Nancy, a young woman with braided hair and enormous round glasses, took the bag and handed it to another woman. "That goes in display case 3B, I think," she said.

The woman carried the bag across a large gymnasium. At the far end, a crew hammered together an information kiosk, while another group hung a banner from the rafters. All the workers were young adults, probably students. This year, the film festival had expanded to include a showroom, with booths dedicated to each movie in the contest. Spark noticed one booth for an amateur western, with a mannequin dressed in a cowboy costume. Another booth, for a science-fiction film, featured a life-size model of an alien.

The overhead lights began to switch off one by one.

"Let's go! We're closing up for the day," a voice shouted.

The woman stopped at the last booth. An easel displayed a poster for the kids' teddy bear movie. Someone—probably Sofia—had photoshopped Spark thrusting her sword at the camera. Behind her, Rana, Amazon Princess™, Ozzie the polar bear, Lulu the panda, and Zed the sock monkey stood ready to fight.

The woman used a key to unlock a glass display case and then dumped the bag inside.

"Let's go, leave that for tomorrow," someone shouted. The woman closed the case and locked it. Spark waited as the people began to file out of the room. Across the aisle, a booth for a romantic movie called *Tender Hearts* featured a poster of a young couple gazing at each other.

Soon the auditorium emptied, and the main doors closed for the day. A single fluorescent light buzzed at the far end of the room. Spark untangled herself from Zed and worked her way out of the plastic bag. She tested the glass case, but the lid would not budge.

Zed whimpered at their predicament. "I was trying to tell you that Loretta wanted to take us to the college," he said. "That was today."

"Yes, I figured that out, Zed. Thank you."

A beam of light suddenly blinded her. Zed screamed.

"I thought I smelled someone familiar," a voice said.

The light flicked off. Three shadowy figures huddled on the other side of the case, behind a plastic divider. The light switched on again. This time, Lulu the panda held a penlight under her chin, casting shadows that stretched to her ears. Ozzie poked his head over her shoulder, his white fur flattened against the glass. And behind him, Rana's blonde hair spilled from her crown, reflecting the light like strands of gold.

"You two make way too much noise to be in the League of Ursus," Lulu said.

Spark couldn't help herself. A giggle bubbled up inside of her, and soon she was doubled over with laughter. She was so happy to see these warriors again. It was the first good news in a long time.

"The juro is still in effect, remember?" Ozzie said. "You have my sword and my life. Until the final light."

"You have my sword and my life," Lulu repeated. "Until the final light."

Unlike the others, Rana had a literal sword, which she pulled from its sheath. "I made you a promise, little bear," she said. "I'm going to do it right this time. You have my sword and my life. Always."

Spark composed herself. She had so much to tell them, and most of it was bad. But for the moment, this ritual brought her a sense of peace.

"I call on all bears to be true," she said, "and I pledge you my life. Until the final light. Until every last monster is defeated."

Everyone turned to Zed. "Oh, lay off," he said. Poor Zed. He was terrible at memorizing the League pledges. "Fine," he said. "Uh, I'll do my best. Okay?"

"I'll take it," Spark said. "Now, Lulu, can you pick this lock?"

Lulu, a master thief, pretended to find this question offensive. "Does a polar bear like snow?"

Spark smiled.

Ozzie leaned closer and said: "A polar bear likes snow."

"Indeed," Spark said. "Let's hurry. There are monsters out there."

THIRTY

While Spark told the juro a short version of everything that had happened, Lulu pulled a pair of bobby pins from a hole under her arm. Spark could only imagine what other tools she kept hidden in her stuffing. For a few tense minutes, the panda tinkered with the latch. Spark could hear plastic catching on metal. Every time the bears crept too close, Lulu shooed them away.

"Gimme some space," she said. "This is more an art than a science."

"But you *can* do it," Spark said.

"From the outside, I woulda had this done in three minutes. Piece o' cake. From the inside, ya gotta finesse it."

She pressed her stubby ear to the plastic and worked by sound alone. While pointing the bobby pins at various angles, she raised and lowered her eyebrows, depending on the vibrations she detected. Spark could never tell when Lulu heard something she liked.

Ozzie still had questions. "So Jakmal *helped* you? I mean, he helped . . . *you.*"

"Look, I don't know if we can trust him—or *them.* Whatever."

"We can't," Lulu said, still listening for the latch to cooperate.

"But we're working toward the same thing. And we have the

same enemies."

"Are we? And do we?" Lulu said.

Spark knelt beside her. "I know you didn't make it this far by trusting monsters," Spark said. "I'm asking you to trust *me*."

"I *do* trust you! But your plan is to break into the Grand Sleuth's headquarters and take the scratcher. And hope the worst monsters ever don't show up."

"Spark summoned the juro," Ozzie reminded Lulu. "And she has made her decision."

"But wait," Rana said, "you said there was a peace treaty."

"I don't recognize their treaty," Spark said. "Look, Agnes and her friends are caught up in something they can't control. So they took the easy way out. But we can do the right thing. The impossible thing."

The latch clicked, and the glass display case snapped open.

"Starting with that," Lulu said.

One at a time they jumped to the floor. From below, the booths and display cases towered over them like a city skyline. The exit sign glowed red in the distance.

"There are still students all over campus," Ozzie said. "We have to be quiet."

"Yeah, if we get caught here, they might take us to the science lab," Zed said, shivering. "For experiments."

"Nobody's going to the science lab," Spark said.

Spark tried to visualize the map that the Grand Sleuth had given her, but it was no use. The map did not cover the college. They were stranded.

"What are your orders?" Lulu said.

"Okay, okay," Spark stammered. "We need a map. Or a computer, or a phone—anything that'll give us directions to the hospital."

Ozzie, trying to be supportive, glanced around at the booths on the slim chance that one might have a map.

"Every college has a computer lab," Rana said. "But it'll be stuffed with students. We can't just walk in."

"We don't have ID," Ozzie said.

"Even if we found a map, how are we gonna get there?" Lulu said.

Spark imagined them trudging through construction sites, forests, backyards. It could take days. On her way here, she had felt the car gliding on a highway, which could prove impossible to cross. In her desperation, she pictured herself pole-vaulting over a four-lane expressway.

"Hey, don't they *take* you to the hospital?" Zed asked.

"Huh?" Spark said.

"I remember Mom called 911 once, and a white truck pulled into the driveway with the lights and sirens going *wee-oo wee-oo*. I hid under the bed, I was so scared."

Spark laughed as she realized she had been overthinking it. "Let's find a phone."

They left the gymnasium and sneaked into an empty office down the hall. While Zed acted as a lookout, the others climbed the desk and gathered around the phone. Unlike the one at home, this phone had a big speaker box and a row of buttons that Spark did not recognize.

"Is this a good idea?" Ozzie asked. "I mean, what if someone out there really needs help and we're taking an ambulance off the streets?"

"Everyone's gonna need an ambulance if we don't get to the hospital right away," Spark said. That answer was good enough for the polar bear.

They decided that Rana would do the talking after agreeing that she had the most human-sounding voice, which she took as a compliment.

"You have that 'I need to speak to your manager' voice," Lulu said.

Rana agreed. "I'll tell them that a student fainted. Right outside the doors."

Spark dialed the number.

"911, what's your emergency?" a man said on the other end.

Rana cleared her throat and began to speak in a hifalutin voice, with an accent that veered from British to French and back again. "Yes, hello, good evening," she said. "This is Professor LeBlanc. I teach *thee*-ya-tah at the college."

"O . . . kay," the dispatcher said.

"You don't have to make up a name!" Spark whispered.

"Just talk normal," Ozzie hissed.

"Yes, a terrible thing," Rana said. "A poor student appears to have fainted near the entrance of the main . . . campus . . . center."

"It's the arts school," Spark whispered. "Just say the arts school."

"Is the person breathing?" the dispatcher said.

"Yes, but please hurry—"

"Is the person injured? Any signs of head trauma?"

"Um . . . no, he just passed out, the poor thing."

"Does he have a medical ID bracelet? Did he take anything prior to passing out?"

Rana balled her plastic hands into fists. She did not expect so many questions. Spark twirled her paw to indicate that she should keep going.

Lulu had a better idea. "Just say you ran into the building to call an ambulance," she whispered.

"Right," Rana said. "I ran straight to my office when I saw him collapse. The young man was breathing when I left. That's all I know. Now can you please send an ambulance right away? Please?"

That was better. Everyone breathed easier for a second.

"All right," the dispatcher said. "What's your exact address?"

Rana froze again. "I don't know."

"Gah!" Spark said. She rifled through the papers on the desk, looking for an envelope or a letter that might have the information. She found a business card and held it up like a picket sign. Rana read the address to the dispatcher, who assured her that an ambulance would arrive soon.

To reach the entrance of the building, the juro jumped out of the office window and worked their way between the wall and a row of shrubs. The sun had set, though it was still bright enough for someone to spot them out in the open. A few students passed on the sidewalk, some in chatty pairs and some silently listening to music on their headphones. The women's track team ran past all at once.

By the time the juro arrived at the glass doors, the parking lot glowed with the twirling red and white lights of an ambulance. Immediately, a security guard intercepted the vehicle. The paramedics stepped out—two muscular men wearing tight navy shirts with white shields on the sleeves. They each snapped on a pair of rubber gloves. One of them pulled an orange nylon bag from the passenger seat.

"Got a call from one of your professors," he said.

"About what?" the security guard said.

This triggered a debate about who called whom, when, and why. Spark saw her chance. She led the juro to the rear of the ambulance. From there, they climbed onto the roof and hid behind the emergency lights.

The radio in the ambulance buzzed, and the paramedics talked with their dispatcher. "Yeah, looks like a prank call," one of them said.

The security guard apologized. "Might've been some kid trying to get into a fraternity or something," he said.

Spark finally relaxed a bit when the two doors shut and the emergency lights switched off. The engine started again.

"Hold on tight," she said. Everyone wrapped their arms around the rack that held the lights.

"Look at that," Rana said.

In the distance, the sky had turned a deep blue, and a purple cloud hung over the town. A flash of lightning rippled through the darkness, and a few seconds later the rumbling arrived at the campus.

"That's weird," Lulu said.

As the ambulance made a U-turn, the security guard caught a glimpse of the stuffed animals hanging onto the lights. The man put his hands on his hips and shook his head, looking disappointed that the paramedics would attach toys to their vehicle. So unprofessional.

A few blocks from campus, the ambulance stopped at a red light. A car pulled close behind and the passenger, a teenage girl, took a photo of the toys sitting on the roof. She giggled and tapped the screen, and Spark imagined the image beaming to millions of other phones. She couldn't do anything about it now.

The ambulance pulled onto the highway, heading directly into the storm. The wind whipped along the sides of the truck. Up close, the cloud looked more textured, with menacing tendrils snaking out of the bottom. As night fell, the cloud became like a tentacled monster descending upon the town.

Minutes later, when the ambulance arrived at the hospital, Spark could no longer deny it. The cloud was spinning directly above the building, an enormous, lumpy disk that grew wider with each revolution. This was no storm. It was a highly unstable portal, made by a hastily built scratcher. Spark and her friends gazed up at the swirling mass as the ambulance pulled up to the crescent-shaped entrance. Spark leapt off the roof and onto the rear bumper. The others followed. They took cover behind the wheels.

"I'm gonna check with Marge," one of the paramedics said. He headed for the doors.

The other one, the driver, leaned on the side of the truck. "What's up with this storm?" he asked.

His colleague shrugged. "No idea. Just hoping it doesn't blow any power lines down." The two glass doors slid open to let him into the building.

With no one around to notice them, Spark gestured for the juro to follow her into the parking garage, where they hid behind a row of smelly trash barrels and planned their next move.

"We'll go through the kitchen to get to the playroom," Spark said.

Outside, another ambulance arrived, and the garage filled with flashing red and white lights. The rear doors opened and a stretcher emerged. A crew of nurses rushed to the vehicle.

"Ozzie and Rana, see if you can grab any weapons. The sharper the better."

She turned to Lulu. "Scope out the playroom. I want to know what the Grand Sleuth is doing."

"Uh, Spark," Zed said.

"There are doctors' offices in the hallway. Find an empty one, and I'll meet you there."

"Spark!" Zed repeated, pointing to the ambulance.

On the stretcher, a girl lay passed out. She was covered by a blanket and had a plastic respirator mask attached to her face. The paramedic shouted a string of jargon at the nurses. Spark couldn't understand any of it.

A man and a woman ran behind them, trying to get a look at the girl. It was . . . it was Mom and Dad! And that meant—

"Loretta!" Spark said.

That was her dusa on the stretcher. Something must have happened at Sofia's basketball game. Everything slowed down. The shouting voices became muffled. The sliding doors opened to let them in. Zed hopped around, unable to contain his panic.

"Just when I thought things couldn't get any worse," he said.

"Spark," Ozzie said, pointing to the parking lot. "It's worse."

Two children jogged toward the building. It was Sofia in the lead, running as fast as she could, her open windbreaker flapping, with Matthew struggling to keep pace. It seemed they had all arrived together.

"That's Sofia!" Lulu said.

"Sofia? As in kidnapped-by-monsters Sofia?" Rana said.

Matthew was hastily buttoning his jean jacket against the stiff wind. The main doors slid apart with a *whoosh* as they entered.

"Karacor did this," Spark said.

Lulu gave her the side-eye. "Karacor?"

"I don't know how. I just have a feeling. He didn't want to go to her. So he made her come to him."

Spark could picture it: the creepy man with the wide smile, hidden among the crowd in the stands. Maybe he wore a hat to conceal himself. He couldn't just kidnap Loretta from the gymnasium. Too risky, despite his immense power. Maybe he placed some kind of spell on her, so she would end up exactly where he needed her.

All the children were here now. And Molly, too! With this portal ripping the sky apart, they were all in danger.

"What do we do now?" Lulu said.

It took everything in Spark's power not to race after Loretta. She told herself to stick to the plan, but her teddy-bear instincts nearly overruled her logic.

"I need to figure out what's going on," she said.

Before they could object, she repeated her orders to gather whatever weapons they could find, stake out the playroom, and lay low until she returned. "And keep an eye out for the smiling man," she said. "You'll know him when you see him. I'll find out where they're taking Loretta."

Lulu nodded. "If you're not back in ten minutes, we're storming that playroom like it's D-Day."

"Agreed."

"What's D-Day?" Zed asked.

"A new video game Darcy has," Lulu said. "You'd like it."

Zed did not seem convinced.

Spark figured that the best way to find Loretta would be through the dining hall, past the playroom, and into the main reception area. This would not be as easy as the last time. In the early evening, more people would be moving about, with the night-shift nurses, doctors, and security guards arriving soon.

But first, she turned to her juro.

"What are you waiting for?" Rana said.

"I'm trying to remember the pledge," Spark said with a laugh. She tried to concentrate, but the words would not come together in her mind.

Rana put her hands on her hips. "Bears serve . . ."

"Right. Bears watch."

And then they all joined in: "Bears protect. Always and forever."

Spark did not want to admit that she was scared. She ran for the dining hall before the feeling could catch up with her.

THIRTY-ONE

In the hallway, a chair stood next to the door of each office, which allowed Spark to hide as she made her way to the reception area. In the worst-case scenario, she would simply keel over and pretend to be a stuffed animal that someone had left on the floor. Whoever found her would hopefully return her to the playroom, where she needed to go anyway at some point. Not a perfect plan, or even a good one, but with the apocalypse churning overhead, she had few options.

Spark remained hidden as a stretcher squeaked by. Then she slunk under a chair in which an elderly patient sat, half asleep, holding his paperwork on his lap. The ambient noise grew louder as Spark approached the lobby, where three nurses in turquoise scrubs worked behind the round reception desk. Phones rang. Sick people coughed in the waiting area. Elevators pinged, their doors rumbling open. Loudspeakers summoned doctors to surgery rooms and intensive care units.

Adding to the chaos, one of the paramedics rolled Loretta's stretcher up to the desk while a nurse signed something on a clipboard and handed it to the receptionists. Dad watched anxiously, his fingers fiddling with the zipper on his jacket. He mouthed the words

Come on while the nurses debated where the stretcher would go. Mom put her arm around Matthew. Under normal circumstances, he would have shrugged her off, thinking himself too old for that kind of thing. But he leaned into her now.

"Did she say anything to you before she passed out?" Mom said.

"No," Matthew said.

"Anything about how she was feeling?"

"No."

"I was coming off the court," Sofia said. "I didn't know anything was wrong until I saw Matthew waving to me from the stands."

The automatic doors swooshed again, and Mr. Lopez stomped inside, still dressed in his khaki work uniform, a plastic ID badge dangling from his front pocket. He stopped when he saw the chaos unfolding. Then he spotted Sofia.

"How did you get here?" he asked.

"They drove me," Sofia said.

Mr. Lopez gave Mom and Dad a look. No doubt he had more to say, but he knew this was not the time. Spark had no reason to like him. And yet seeing him like this, she realized that he was simply a scared man, maybe in over his head, always trying his best and never knowing if it was good enough. Mom and Dad must have felt that way, too, sometimes.

"Let's go," he said, reaching for Sofia's hand.

"No!"

"We're leaving."

"Dad, I wanna know if Loretta's okay."

Matthew stepped forward. "Mr. Lopez, I asked her to come along—"

"Didn't I tell you to stay away from us? Didn't I?"

"You don't need to talk to him like that," Dad said as calmly as he could. "If there's a problem, you can talk to me."

Realizing that he had gone too far, Mr. Lopez backed off. "I'm sorry. I hope Loretta's okay. But we're leaving."

"No, we're not!" Sofia said.

While they argued, Matthew gave them space. Meanwhile, the nurses wheeled the stretcher toward the hallway. Spark shimmied farther under the chair as the wheels rolled past her. The loudspeaker blasted another announcement: "Dr. Kitzman, you're needed in main reception. Dr. Kitzman to main reception."

As they took Loretta away, Spark wanted so badly to connect with her dusa the way Agnes had shown her, if only to let her know she was not alone. Spark closed her eyes and tried to concentrate. In her mind, she re-created Loretta's room, filling in every detail down to the softness of the rug and the cobwebs in the corner. The image would not last, however. The chatter in the lobby kept bringing Spark back to this spot, where she felt so far away from everything she loved.

Spark could not wait here forever. She tore herself from the lobby and hurried back to the doctors' offices, where the juro would regroup. In this part of the building, the noise from the reception area dwindled to a low murmur. On the walls, flyers and posters showed how to perform the Heimlich maneuver, where to get vaccinated, and how to detect the signs of a heart attack.

"Psst!" someone said. A furry white paw stuck out from one of the doorways, waving her over. Spark waited for two orderlies to cross the intersection down the hall. Once they were gone, she zipped across the floor and dove into the office, where a row of medical certificates in gold frames hung on the wall.

Ozzie led Spark to the other side of the desk, where she found Zed and Rana hiding. So far, they had collected a set of scalpels, a fire extinguisher that only Ozzie could lift, and a plastic box with brightly colored buttons on it.

"Defibrillator," Rana said. "You could zap a monster with that."

The door creaked. Lulu had returned. As if in a daze, the panda waddled toward the desk, staring into space, her mouth hanging open in disbelief.

"Where's the Grand Sleuth?" Spark asked.

"Gone," Lulu said absently. "There are no bears in the playroom. Just a few spaceships and G.I. Joes."

The bears grew tense at the news. Agnes and the others must have known something huge was about to happen.

"But we've got bigger problems," Lulu said.

"What's wrong?"

"The lobby."

"I just came from there," Spark began—and then she noticed that the low murmur of voices was gone. The hospital was dead silent. She signaled for the juro to follow her. Ozzie took the fire extinguisher, Rana the defibrillator, and Lulu a scalpel. Zed took a scalpel too, though the awkward way he held it did not inspire much confidence.

In single file, the juro entered the hallway. Spark went first, running to the next doorframe and taking cover. At the other end of the hall, nothing moved. The silence felt thick. Spark reached the lobby entrance and stuck her head around the corner. A man in scrubs stood perfectly still, staring right at her. She pulled back and signaled for the others to wait. Slowly, she tried again. The man was still there, eyes open, one hand holding a paper coffee cup, the other a clipboard.

Spark took a few more steps, and the lobby widened around her. Everyone in the room was completely still. Two security officers had frozen in midsentence while chatting. Spark recognized their faces—it was Mustache and Rookie from the other night. A few feet away, a receptionist held a receiver to her ear, but her mouth was clamped shut. A tinny voice on the other end said, "Hello? Hello?" A second phone rang on the desk, right in front of another receptionist who just sat there while the little red light blinked. Near the entrance, a doctor was stuck midstride.

Spark's heart sank when she saw her family in the waiting area. Sofia and Matthew had gone stiff as well. Spark waited for them to move, but they wouldn't. It was like they were posing for an awkward picture.

Someone needed to say the obvious. "It must be a spell," Spark said. When Jak kidnapped Matthew, he cast a similar one—a muffle, Sir Reginald had called it—that made it so that humans could not hear him. This spell, whatever its name, was far worse. Cast by someone far more powerful.

The phone stopped ringing. Outside, the wind blew harder, pelting the windows with leaves and twigs. The storm cloud now expanded all the way to the horizon. Though there wasn't a drop of rain, the cloud appeared ready to flood the entire town at any second. Thick vapor descended into the parking lot, fogging over the lamps. Soon, the air looked like milk poured into coffee. Darkness swallowed everything.

Someone whimpered. Spark realized that it may have been her.

Lightning flashed, and a single figure appeared in the parking lot. "Hide!" Spark yelled.

The bears scattered. Spark and Ozzie dashed behind a pillar near the door. Lulu and Rana went for the desk. Zed, in his panic, took cover at the feet of one of the frozen doctors.

The figure outside drew closer. It was Karacor. No one needed to ask.

The wind died down, allowing his long black coat to rest against his thin frame. He wore a silvery dress shirt tucked into pleated slacks. His patent leather shoes clicked on the asphalt. Another flash of lightning painted his bald head completely white. With his oddly serene expression, he resembled a man taking a nice stroll on a warm spring day. Not a care in the world. That was what scared Spark the most.

"Look!" Lulu said.

Spark watched as the Grand Sleuth marched into the parking lot, single file, with Agnes leading the way. They had hidden behind the dumpsters like a pack of raccoons, waiting for the smiling man to arrive. Agnes leaned on her cane. Behind her, Mason held an object in both paws: a metal tube, a few inches long, with a blinking red light on it.

"That's our scratcher," Spark said.

Iggy marched behind them, followed by the rest of the bears, the brown and black ones, the bright-blue and red ones. Together they looked like a victory parade.

"Hold on," Lulu said. "That's Sir Reginald!"

At the end of the line, a bear with weathered black fur stood at attention alongside the others. The sword Arctos dangled from his belt.

Spark felt as if she could tip right over. "That's Reggie." Agnes must have tricked this sweet bear, feeding him lies about duty and honor, all to gain some kind of advantage over Spark's juro. Or simply to be cruel.

"He's not one of them," Ozzie said. "Is he?"

"No," Spark said firmly. Everyone knew not to argue with her.

With the two dozen or so bears formed in a neat little line before him, Karacor sniffed the air. He walked from one end of the row to the other like a general inspecting his troops. His nose wrinkled when he made it to pink bear.

"My old friend," he said, his voice as delicate and smooth as a child's. "In all this excitement, I forgot to ask you something."

"Go ahead," she said.

"What do the humans call you now?"

"Agnes."

"How sweet. Named after someone's grandmother, I suppose." He turned his attention to the blinking device in Mason's paws. "You know, Agnes. It would be most unfortunate if your scratcher fails to work."

"Look around you," Mason said. "It works."

Without raising his head, the man glanced at the clouds. "Primitive. A scratcher should be a little more . . . discreet. But this will do."

Agnes looked uneasy.

"Do not be troubled," the man said. "We have secured the peace." He crouched down close enough for her to smell his breath. "Imagine how awful it would be if you did not have the wisdom to see this through."

"It would be awful for both of us," Agnes said coldly.

Karacor twirled his fingers, a signal for them to get on with it. Mason furiously tapped the buttons on his pawheld device. The lights on the side blinked. The storm cloud spun faster.

"All right, that's our target," Spark said, pointing at the mini scratcher. "We have to get that thing out of Mason's hands."

Ozzie counted the bears. "He's surrounded. There are too many of them."

Several of the bears had peeled away from the others so they could act as lookouts.

"We could take out the guards," Lulu said. "You try to punch through. Maybe Zed can jump for the scratcher."

"Wait," Ozzie said. "There's more."

Spark expected to see another group of bears. Instead, a lumbering monster with demon-like wings trudged across the parking lot.

Its entire body was the same gray color, like granite. Another just like it emerged from the abandoned wing. It turned its head toward the hospital, and Spark ducked—but not before seeing its smooth eyes, like stones found on a beach.

"Oh, no," Spark said.

She recognized them as the angel statues guarding the old hospital wing, the ones she passed by when she followed the children inside. More creatures appeared, marching in single file from the abandoned building. Spark counted ten of them. One was a skinny sticklike figure with arms so long they dragged on the ground. Then came a squat, furry creature with a pig nose and two horns on its head. Bringing up the rear was the creepy skeleton sculpture that hung on the lobby wall. It shambled toward the portal, its bones clinking like broken wind chimes.

They had been here this entire time, hiding in the basement where the children were too afraid to go. The monsters had not merely surrounded the Grand Sleuth, as Agnes had said. They held the Grand Sleuth hostage!

The swirling cloud descended toward the ground like a tornado. One by one, the monsters stepped into the funnel and vanished. The portal made a sound as they entered. *Shoonk! Shoonk!* Like a vacuum cleaner sucking up dirt. Agnes seemed pleased with herself, standing before her loyal soldiers. She had kept the peace. She had saved the Grand Sleuth and protected her dusa.

All Karacor had to do was step into the portal with his friends. If he did that, then Spark could go home without a fight. Instead, he turned to Agnes, the smile stretching his gaunt face.

"You have been most kind," he said. "There is one last favor I'd like to ask."

Agnes snorted. "You're the only one left. Now is not the time to change the deal." She laughed, and the other bears joined in.

"The portal is still open." Karacor's meaning was clear: he could summon his friends from the other side. Mason, clearly trying not to panic, tapped the buttons on his scratcher. But this portal was unstable. Karacor was negotiating from a position of strength.

"Agnes, please," Karacor said. "It's just a small favor. Between old friends."

"Name it, then," Agnes said.

"You have something that I want. I think you know what I'm talking about."

Mason turned to Agnes, waiting for her answer.

"The *girl*," Karacor said.

Agnes did not move, did not even blink. Spark had told her the truth and Agnes refused to listen. Now it was too late.

"All right," Spark said. "I've seen enough."

"Tell me you have an elaborate plan," Rana said.

"It's not elaborate," Spark said. "It's brute force. Now let's get to the garage."

They fell in behind her, making sure to stay low so the lookouts wouldn't spot them. As they left the lobby, Spark took one last look down the hallway where they had taken Loretta. Spark would die for this girl. She would start a war to save her. No peace would be worth her dusa's life.

"Spark, let's go!" Ozzie said.

She ran to him, imagining herself as the full-sized grizzly from the paintings in Jak's castle.

"Let's go to war!" she shouted.

THIRTY-TWO

"So, you didn't actually *drive* the car," Rana said.

The Amazon Princess™ had wedged herself under the driver's seat of the ambulance. She pressed her right boot on the gas pedal, her left on the brake. Ozzie sat on the seat above her, his two paws gripping the lower part of the steering wheel. Perched on his shoulders, Spark took the top of the wheel. From there, she could see above the dashboard to the garage entrance and the parking lot outside.

"Well, I sort of drove it," Spark said.

"You *rolled* it," Ozzie said.

"Right, I rolled it—"

"That doesn't mean you drove it!" Rana said. "I could roll anything. I could drop a toy car down a flight of steps. That doesn't mean I *drove* it."

"We can figure this out," Spark said. "How hard can it be?"

"I guess we'll find out," Rana grumbled.

At least the driver had left the key in the ignition. He was frozen just a few feet away. Spark reached for it and prepared to give it a turn. "Everyone ready?"

Ozzie pulled the seatbelt over his chest and clicked it into place.

In the backseat, Lulu sat on top of a cabinet full of medical supplies. Zed crouched beside her, trying his best to contain his fear. They both nodded to Spark in the rearview mirror.

"I guess I'm ready," Rana said. They had decided that her hard boots would work best for pressing the pedals. Ozzie would help steer as well as operate the gearshift, and Spark would navigate.

She tried to turn the key but found it locked. Ozzie tried to help. After some trial and error, they figured out that they needed to press the ignition and then turn. Once they did, the engine roared to life.

With the steering wheel vibrating under her paws, Spark signaled to Ozzie. The polar bear grabbed the gearshift and jerked it toward the floor. On the dashboard, a red plastic pin moved from the letter P to the letter R. They had debated what the R stood for. When the ambulanced rolled backward, Spark realized that it meant reverse.

"One more, Ozzie!" she said. "Quick!"

The rear bumper hit the back wall of the garage.

Ozzie shifted to the letter N, which didn't seem to do anything, and then to D, which had a bright white circle around it. The ambulance lurched forward.

"That's it!" Spark said. "All right, Rana, give us some gas."

Rana timidly tapped the pedal. The engine revved, but the ambulance merely limped forward before rolling back again.

"Punch it!" Spark said.

"I'm punching it!"

Alerted by the sound of the engine, one of Agnes's bodyguards appeared in the entrance, a stout brown bear with worn elbows and knees and only one eye. He had a whistle tied around his neck so he could call the others.

"Rana, this is no time to obey traffic laws!" Spark yelled. "Now gimme everything!"

"Hey!" the bodyguard shouted, fumbling with the whistle.

Rana slammed the pedal to the floor. Spark's head tilted back as the van accelerated. She flicked on the headlights. The one-eyed bear lifted a paw to shield his face right before the front tire collided with him. The ambulance shuddered.

"What was that?" Ozzie shouted.

"Speed bump," Spark said.

In the sideview mirror, Spark saw the flattened bear pat himself back into shape. He did not look happy.

"Now help me turn right," she said to Ozzie.

All four of their paws pulled the wheel to the right as the ambulance burst out of the garage. Rubber squealed against asphalt. Spark felt her body lean toward the side window as she aimed the vehicle at the Grand Sleuth. The smiling man stayed still while the teddies scrambled about, trying to avoid the oncoming danger. Reggie fled toward the building, and Spark swerved around him. Another bear ran in the opposite direction, holding a blinking object in his paw.

Lulu shouted, "There he is! There's Mason!"

"I see him," Spark said. "Get ready."

Zed and Lulu opened the rear doors, which flapped outward like wings.

"Left a little," Spark said, and Ozzie turned the wheel slightly.

Mason ran through the crowd, shoving aside another bear before finding himself directly in the path of the oncoming van. He dropped to his stomach as the ambulance passed over him. Which was exactly what they wanted him to do.

"Now, Lulu!"

Lulu grabbed the rear bumper with one hand while holding Zed's tail with the other. Once the ambulance passed over Mason, Zed hopped out and landed on top of him. Lulu then yanked on the monkey's tail, pulling both of them off the ground. They rose in the air and landed on the bumper, while Mason struggled to break free.

Spark watched through the rearview mirror—and then realized

she was about to drive into the fence at the end of the parking lot.

"Right! Turn right!"

The ambulance tilted. Spark and Ozzie spun the wheel as far as it would go, until the van turned completely around. "Straighten it out. Ease up on the gas."

"We're going back?" Ozzie said.

Most of the bears had run away in a panic, with the rest trying to regroup. A few others helped their comrades off the ground. Behind them, Agnes waved her cane and shouted for the bears to attack. Off to the side, Karacor continued to smile, no doubt enjoying the spectacle.

Spark squeezed the wheel. "Punch it again, Rana!"

A sudden jolt, a squeal of tires, and the ambulance charged forward. Ozzie found the switch for the siren, and the parking lot filled with spinning lights and an ear-splitting howl. "Safety first," he said.

"How are we doing back there?" Spark yelled. She checked the rearview mirror. Lulu and Zed scuffled with Mason, trying to pry the scratcher from his paws.

"Brake!" Spark yelled.

Rana kicked in the pedal. Spark braced herself against the steering wheel. The sudden stop sent Mason, Zed, and Lulu flying forward, where they collided with the cabinet. The blinking scratcher hit the floor and skittered all the way to the front seat.

"Gas!" Spark said. Rana stood on the gas pedal, and the tires squealed.

"You fools!" Mason shouted. "You have no idea what—"

"Oh, shut up!" Lulu said. She took a running start and kicked him right in the chest, punting him out of the ambulance and onto the ground, where he landed face-first.

"We got it!" Zed shouted as he held the scratcher aloft.

The ambulance sped past the smiling man and the old pink bear.

Spark made sure to give them a nice side-eye. The man squinted back. To taunt him, Spark blasted the horn. Agnes flinched.

"We did it!" Ozzie said.

"Brute force, baby!" Lulu shouted.

"*Grand* Sleuth," Zed said. "More like *bland*—"

Suddenly, something huge crashed into the windshield from above, caving in the glass. Everyone screamed.

"What's happening?" Rana shouted.

Spark thought the storm had tossed a tree branch at them. But this branch moved. And through the cracks in the glass, Spark saw a pair of bright-red eyes, then two more opening beneath them. And a hinged jaw yawning open. A mangler!

Everyone screamed even louder.

"Brake!" Spark yelled.

It was too late. The ambulance was careening toward the row of dumpsters. Spark and Ozzie cranked the wheel to the left. The odor of burnt tire singed her nose. All she could do was hold on while the ambulance crashed, sending the creature flying off the windshield. The sound of metal crunching and twisting seemed to last forever, until it gave way to the whistle of steam leaking from the engine.

Spark lifted her head off the wheel. The mangler popped out of the dumpster, staring right at her, its red eyes glowing in the head-lights.

"Everybody run!" Spark said. "Abandon ship!"

"Run?" Rana said, still hidden underneath the dashboard.

The mangler leapt onto the hood, jostling the ambulance with its enormous weight. Rana stopped asking questions and sprinted to the back. Ozzie unclicked the seatbelt and he and Spark followed suit. The mangler pounded on the remains of the windshield, determined to smash through.

Just outside the ambulance, Zed and Lulu had stopped dead in their tracks, transfixed by the madness taking place outside. The storm had become a twisting column of vapor—a giant, unstable portal spinning like a top over the parking lot. A creepy groan cut through the wind. Hideous forms fell from the cloud, the twisted bodies of manglers landing on the ground, raising their heads, scanning this new environment. They gathered around Karacor like a pack of wolves. He reached out his pale hand and stroked the forehead of one of the beasts.

It was just like the pictures Molly had drawn. She had seen it coming. How could she not? She and her bear were connected. Agnes lived in fear of this very thing, and she had passed that fear on to her dusa.

The remaining bears of the Grand Sleuth ran away, terrified. Their leader was nowhere to be seen.

Spark wanted to scream Agnes's name, to make her come out and beg forgiveness for what she had done. But before she could say anything, the mangler on the hood burst through the windshield.

"Come on!" Spark said, urging the juro to follow her to the hospital. As they ran across the parking lot, the manglers ignored them, choosing instead to fawn over their master. The monster on the ambulance sniffed around for the bears, then lost interest and joined its comrades, forming an army that had never been seen on this planet. Not since the last time, anyway.

The juro made it to the lobby entrance, where the humans remained frozen. As more monsters fell from the sky, Spark ripped the scratcher from Zed's hand.

"We have to shut it off!" she said. She tapped the buttons, and a new portal formed in front of her, a spinning black void that expanded to the size of a beach ball. She let go of the button and it vanished, like soap bubble bursting.

Someone tugged at her shoulder. It was Ozzie. He nodded toward the parking lot. While Spark had been fussing with the scratcher, the manglers had formed into a solid wall, crouched and ready to attack. A row of bright-red eyes stared back at her.

Karacor lifted his right hand. When he snapped his fingers, the manglers charged at once, galloping on all fours, a phalanx of fangs and claws that would bring about the final light.

THIRTY-THREE

The ground rumbled as the manglers charged. The automatic doors would soon open to let them in.

Spark had only a second to think. She looked above the doorframe and saw a tiny plastic box—the sensor that opened the door. The doctor was still stuck just inside the entrance, stiff as a mannequin.

"Zed!" Spark cried, pointing to the sensor. "Smash that thing! Hurry!"

Zed climbed up the doctor's back and bounded off his shoulder. He grabbed the plastic box and punched it three times until the little glass eye inside cracked. The two doors slid into place and sealed shut as Zed dropped to the ground.

The first monster slammed into the glass with a bang so loud that Spark could feel it in her chest. Zed let out a piercing shriek and scampered behind her.

More manglers collided with the barrier, their mouths opening and their teeth scraping against the glass. Some were so eager to get inside that they crawled atop their comrades. The building's architects must have designed the doors to withstand a hurricane or earthquake. The glass would not shatter. It would not hold forever, though.

"New plan," Spark said. "We need to get Loretta as far from here as we can." She noticed a motorized chair parked in the waiting area. Spark hopped onto the armrest and used the joystick to steer across the lobby, snaking around the frozen humans. The others ran alongside her.

"What about the other children?" Ozzie said.

"She's the one they want. Come on!"

Rana adjusted her crown. "How much time do we have until that portal . . . ya know?"

They all knew what she meant: until it became so huge that the fabric between the two worlds tore apart completely, never to be repaired.

"Can't be long now," Spark said.

"We could try to give the scratcher back," Rana said. "Then they can—"

"No! Don't say it." Spark emphasized each word by shaking the device in Rana's direction. "This is the only leverage we have! We can't just—"

Glass shattered somewhere in the building. Spark was trying to locate the sound when something thudded on the level above them.

"They're on the second floor," Ozzie said.

A set of footsteps—too heavy for a human—galloped across the ceiling. The overhead fluorescent lights flickered under the weight, their plastic covers rattling.

"Where's Loretta's room?" Spark asked.

"Somewhere down this hallway," Ozzie said.

Spark drove the wheelchair past the reception desk. She sent Lulu ahead. The panda kicked open three doors before finding the right one.

Spark parked the wheelchair beside Loretta's bed. Her dusa lay still, her eyes closed, her head rolled to one shoulder. It took the juro's combined strength to push her onto the chair, where she flopped like a ragdoll. They adjusted her legs and feet until she was sitting upright. While Spark drove the chair down the hall, Ozzie and Lulu took the lead with Zed and Rana protecting the rear. Together, their little convoy looked like the Secret Service protecting the presidential limousine.

They passed the radiology department, the neonatal ward, the burn unit. Somewhere in the building, the manglers shrieked as they searched for the girl. It sounded at first like a plea for help. But as the wheelchair moved deeper into the building, their screams took on a more threatening tone.

Finally, the juro reached an illuminated red EXIT sign. A placard below warned that an alarm would sound if they opened the door.

Ozzie got nervous. "Maybe we shouldn't—"

Too late—the motorized wheelchair pushed open the door, tripping a fire alarm that echoed throughout the building. There was no point in hiding now. The monsters would find them soon enough. Their only hope was to outrun them.

The chair rolled onto the loading dock and down the ramp. From there, Spark steered across the rear lot toward the fence. On the other side was the park, where they might have a chance to scatter in the darkness. But when Spark searched for a gate, she realized that the fence extended a full block in both directions.

"Now what?" Rana said.

Spark tried to remember the map that the Grand Sleuth had given her. "Let's go left," she said.

As soon as she managed to spin the wheelchair in a new direction, an object appeared in their path—a lump of fur. One of Agnes's minions. The bear stepped forward into the amber light, hesitant but determined to stop these rogues from escaping. He wore a plastic whistle on a string around his neck. Spark recognized the sharp

197

snout, the beady marble eyes, the thick paws.

"Sir Reginald!" Zed gasped.

"Reggie," Spark said.

"I'm arresting you in the name of the Grand Sleuth," Reggie said, his voice shaking. "You will answer for your crimes."

He sounded more like the old Sir Reginald, which made it even worse.

Spark hopped down from the armrest and walked toward him, extending her paws so the others would step aside. "I don't know what they've told you, but we are not your enemy."

"You betrayed the Grand Sleuth," Reggie said.

"Okay, you're right," Spark said. "We did betray the Grand Sleuth."

"Spark!" Ozzie said.

"No," she said. "Agnes told you the truth."

Reggie lifted the whistle to his mouth.

"But they wanted *you* to betray your dusa."

Reggie stopped. "Jared is my dusa. Agnes told me that you put him in danger."

Of course, Spark thought. Agnes manipulated him the same way Karacor had manipulated her.

"Jared is your dusa, I know," she said. "But I also know that you remember things. You remember your old life. Before the final light."

"Agnes said there is no final light. She said you would try to scare me."

Reggie tugged on his whistle. Spark needed him to keep talking.

"You remember Matthew, don't you?" she said.

"You're trying to trick me."

"No tricks. You saw him, right? Inside the hospital." *Please say yes*, she thought.

"Maybe," he said.

"You saw the shirt he was wearing. It's his favorite shirt. He wears it on special occasions."

"His shirt?"

"Please, Reggie," Spark said. "If you remembered all those symbols you drew on the wall, you must remember this. It's the shirt that says Young Filmmakers Award on the front."

Reggie thought for a few seconds. "I remember what a scratcher is," he said. "Let me see it."

Spark glanced at the others. No one seemed ready to tell her what to do. Ozzie managed a shrug.

When she turned to Reggie again, the bear held the whistle in his mouth.

"Reggie, listen to me—"

The whistle blew, a noise so loud that Spark's ears twitched. She stood as frozen as the humans, her shock so complete that she hardly noticed when Reggie, the ghost of her mentor, pulled the scratcher from her paws.

"Reggie, be careful with that!" Spark said.

Zed darted away from the group, only to stop dead when a wave of manglers rounded the corner of the building. More arrived on the other side. Striding above all of them was Karacor, his monsters streaming past him. Dozens more appeared on the roof, having dropped from the portal. Like a column of ants, they marched down the walls until the building resembled an overflowing fountain.

The manglers formed a snarling barricade around the juro, their breath filling the air with the stench of rotten eggs. Meanwhile, Spark maintained eye contact with Reggie, who let the whistle fall from his mouth and dangle from its string.

"Come on, Sir Reginald!" Lulu said. "You're gonna side with these guys? I mean, look at that creep with the smile on his face!"

Karacor grinned even wider.

"There is no universe in which he's the good guy!" Lulu said.

"*Good* guy," the man said. The manglers grew quiet at the sound of his silky voice. "You still think there are good guys out there?"

"Yeah, us!" Ozzie said.

The man shook his head. "Someday you'll understand. There are monsters. There are victims. And there are people on both sides who make sure things don't get out of hand. Like Agnes and me."

"And where is Agnes?" Spark said.

"She probably didn't want to watch what's about to happen."

Spark pointed at him. "You may have scared *her*, but you don't scare us! We've seen bigger monsters than you—"

The man's jaw dropped open, the bottom part resting on his chest. A sound like thousands of children crying emanated from the gaping chasm where his mouth should have been. He tilted his head back, snapping his jaw shut with a click of his teeth.

"I am not debating a teddy bear," the man said. "Now, you can walk away. But if I hear one more word, my mangler will rip your head off."

The monster at his feet perked up. A line of drool spilled out from its teeth.

"Now listen, little black bear," Karacor said to Reggie. "Are you sure these hoodlums are your friends?"

"Not really," Reggie said.

"I'm not your friend, but I'm not your enemy either. I'm just telling you the truth. These bears tried to ruin our peace agreement. They put your dusa in danger."

Reggie looked at Spark.

"Yes, I know all about Jared," Karacor said. "If you want him to be safe, step aside and let us have the girl."

The manglers cleared a path for Reggie, all the way to the

outstretched arms of their leader.

"Hey, Reggie!" Spark shouted. "Why did Matthew wear his favorite shirt?"

"I warned you, little bear," the man said. He snapped his fingers, and the mangler closest to him began marching toward her.

In a panic, Spark hastily assembled what she figured would be her last words. "He wore it to impress Sofia! He's gonna tell her any day now how he feels. You know it!"

The smiling man clapped his hands, and the mangler beside him broke into a run.

Spark held out her paws, for all the good that would do. As the monster closed in, a tiny dot formed in the air right in front of her. Like the pupil of an eye, it suddenly expanded into a large black circle floating a few inches above the ground.

The mangler saw it and tried to stop by digging in its claws. But it was too late. The creature slid into the floating void and disappeared. Everyone gasped.

When Spark lowered her paws, the first thing she noticed was Reggie, pointing the scratcher at the new portal like a remote control. With a knitted brow and scrunched snout, he looked like the old bear she remembered. He glanced at her, almost as if to say, *You happy now, Hotshot?*

Spark walked around to the other side of the portal. She could hear the creature groaning from within. Then the sound stopped. After a long pause, the limp body of the mangler flew out, ejected from the portal with unspeakable force. It landed at Karacor's feet.

A hideous, spindly leg thrust out of the portal, its claw scraping on asphalt. Then came another. And another. An enormous scaly creature forced its way out—a scorpion body with a man's torso attached.

The monster called Jak rose to his full height. On his chest, the face of Mal hissed at the manglers, warning them to stay away.

The cursed brothers sent the manglers into a frenzy. They slithered and stalked about, howling and snarling. Karacor tried to maintain calm by stroking the ones that came near him. But they awaited an order from their master—only that could satisfy them.

The man's smile faded and his mouth formed a flat line on his pale face.

"Kill it," he said.

THIRTY-FOUR

No human would ever see it. No history book would ever record it. But what happened in that mundane setting—the rear parking lot between the hospital and the chain-link fence—had never before occurred in this world. Jak and Mal, the fallen warriors, leapt from the nightmares of children and charged at the horde of monstrosities, bringing with them all the rage they had carried for centuries. The collision felt like an earthquake.

Jak trampled the first two manglers who dared to form the front line of the attack. The rest rushed in around him like floodwater drowning a valley. Jak's forked tail whipped to one side, sweeping a group of manglers off their feet. The claw at the end grabbed one of the monsters by the neck before it could escape. The tail lifted the creature and then crashed it down onto the others.

To gain higher ground, the manglers climbed onto one another and formed a kind of living siege tower, with those at the top hacking and slashing. Using his powerful arms, Jak plucked off a creature and tossed it aside, only to have another take its place.

Spark and her friends steered Loretta away from the melee, stopping at the fence. Meanwhile, the funnel cloud spread wider, creating the largest portal anyone had ever seen. As it spun, more monsters tumbled out like horrible fruits falling from a rotten tree. They came in different forms, pulled from various nightmare worlds. Some had horns, two heads, tentacles. The moment the bears had dreaded, the moment the humans could have never imagined, had arrived at last. A rift so huge that no one could seal it, cracking open the shell of this world and draining the life inside.

A few of the manglers tumbled away from the fight and turned their attention to the juro. They paced around their prey, wary of the bears but still willing to test them. Reggie stepped forward, brandishing his sword. Ozzie, Rana, and Lulu joined him, if only to give the monsters more targets to choose from. Armed only with medical equipment, they formed a barrier around Loretta.

"You remember how to swing that sword?" Lulu asked.

"I remember everything," Reggie said.

Ozzie placed himself at the center of the line, wielding the fire extinguisher. He pulled the trigger, and a stream of white powder blasted out of the hose. The manglers backed away. "Jakmal's buying us some time," Ozzie said.

Time to do what, Spark had no idea. Desperate, she hopped onto Loretta's lap and grabbed the girl by the collar. "Please!" Spark pleaded. "We need you!" But Loretta would not wake up.

A thunderous boom ripped through the air. On top of the hospital, an enormous mangler had landed, its body thicker than a car, its limbs longer than tree branches.

"Loretta!" Spark said. "You know my voice! It's *your* voice! Please—"

A sudden dizziness overtook her, and she nearly fell over. Spark tried to hold on to Loretta's shirt, but her paw slipped. She hit the ground—no, she hit the *floor*, a carpeted floor. She was back in Loretta's room. It was daytime. A breeze gently lifted the curtains. Loretta was sitting at her desk, tinkering with the editing software

204

on her computer. She spun in her chair to face Spark and gave her a knowing look, as if to say, *I've been expecting you.*

Spark blinked in disbelief and found herself once more in the parking lot, with monsters falling all around her.

"I did it," she whispered.

"Did what?" Rana said, aiming her sword at a mangler that hissed at her.

Spark felt woozy, like she did when Agnes had first shown her this secret. She held onto Loretta's shirt as she waited for everything to stop spinning.

As the fog cleared, an idea took root in her mind. Maybe Loretta had planted it there.

"Zed, get over here!" Spark shouted.

The monkey poked his head out from behind Loretta's wheel-chair.

"You're the fastest," she said. "Go into that portal!"

She pointed to the black circle still hovering a few yards away. Zed shook his head.

"Get Jak's scratcher! Bring it back here!"

"We don't need the scratcher!" Lulu said. "We're trying to *seal* the portal, not create another one!"

Zed nodded desperately in agreement.

"No," Spark said. "We're creating an even bigger portal. And we need both devices to do it."

"Bigger?" Zed squeaked.

"You said you wanted to be in the League, Zed," Spark said. "I believed you! I still do! Now you have to find it in yourself to—"

Before she could finish, the monkey darted toward the portal. He didn't need another speech. He just needed orders. As he zipped past the first few manglers, one of them lazily swiped at him and missed. This monkey was of little interest to them. They let him go.

"What do *we* do?" Lulu said.

"Hold them off!"

"Hold them off?!"

Spark turned to Loretta once more. Again, she shook the girl by her collar. "Loretta? Can you hear me? Loretta . . ."

The sky brightened. Spark shielded her eyes and found herself in Loretta's room on a sunny spring day. She let it settle in around her. Everything smelled fresh and new. Loretta had opened the windows for the first time since winter. Now she waited in her chair, focused on Spark, who lay on her side at the base of the shelf. Instinctively, Spark held still. Even in this dreamworld, she knew the rules: don't move until a human looks away.

But those rules didn't apply anymore. Not now, not with the end of the world on their doorstep. Whatever the risk, Spark needed to stand before her dusa and speak to her as an equal. It was the only way.

Spark propped herself on her elbows and rose onto her feet. Instead of fainting from terror or fleeing the room, Loretta merely smiled, as if she had expected this all along.

Spark walked closer to her friend, and with each step she felt warmth blooming inside of her—just like when Mom and Dad first placed her in Loretta's crib, a sensation she thought she had lost now that Loretta was starting to move on. Time did not exist in the same way here. Past and present melded together.

"We need your help," Spark said. Her first words ever to her dusa—the first ever spoken to her face.

Loretta slid out of her chair and stood. "I know," she said.

A great force shook the house. The wind whipped the curtains, and a cloud blotted out the sun. Loretta's subconscious must have detected that trouble was brewing in the real world.

"These monsters want you because of some power you have,"

Spark said. "I don't exactly understand it. But it's our only hope right now. Karacor thinks it's a power to create. Jak and Mal think it's a power to heal. I'm not sure."

"I might be able to do something," Loretta said. "But I can't do it alone."

Of course, Spark thought. Loretta had said that she felt safer and stronger with her friends around. That was why monsters relied on separating people, isolating them, turning them against one another. But when good people joined forces, the monsters didn't stand a chance.

"Wait," Spark said. This could be her only chance to speak with Loretta. She needed to make it count.

"I just wanted to say," she began, "I am so proud of you."

The house shook again.

"Someday soon, you're gonna have a lot of people telling you who you're supposed to be," Spark said. "But that's for you to decide. No one else. And I know you'll do the right thing."

Loretta knelt beside her bear. "Thank you for always looking out for me," she said.

Loretta lifted Spark by her arm. She hugged the bear tight against her chest, something she had not done in a long time.

"Let's go find our friend," she said.

She carried Spark to the door and opened it. But instead of leading into the hallway, it led into another room—a child's room, with a small bed lined with stuffed animals, crayon drawings taped to the walls, and a three-story dollhouse near the closet.

The room swayed a bit to one side, then to the other. Each time, Spark could hear water sloshing like waves against the hull of a ship. A plastic cup on a miniature table fell over, spilling its imaginary tea. This was Molly's room. And sure enough, she found the girl in her pirate's hat, spinning the wheel of her ship. Molly held her course while pulling a telescope from her coat pocket. She extended the tube and peered through the lens out to the horizon, where a storm front darkened the sky and troubled the sea.

Agnes had told her that by connecting with Loretta, she could connect to all the Grand Sleuth bears—and their dusas. It was true!

When the girl saw Loretta, she collapsed the telescope and shoved it back in her pocket.

Loretta set Spark on the floor just as a heavy wave rocked the ship.

"Molly, I'm a friend of Agnes," Spark said.

"I remember," Molly said. "You're the ship's cook!"

"That's right," Spark said. "Loretta tells me you can help her."

"She can," Loretta said. "But not from here."

She offered her hand to Molly.

"I don't wanna go," Molly said. "I'm waiting for Agnes to come back. We're going sailing together."

Loretta looked to Spark for help.

"I'm sorry, Molly," Spark said. "Agnes is not coming back."

"But she's my first mate," Molly said.

"I know," Spark said. "She told me you were an explorer."

Molly shrugged. "Sure."

"That's why you like being a pirate. So you can sail the high seas. See the world."

"We're *good* pirates, though," Molly said. She was not ready yet. She crossed her arms and turned to the window. Outside, a foamy wave swelled against the horizon.

"It's time for you to wake up," Loretta said. "We're gonna help you. And then *you* can help *us*."

"Help *you*?" Molly said.

"I told you once that I feel stronger when my friends are around. You're my friend."

"It'll be a new adventure," Spark said. "For good pirates."

Molly gazed at the ship's wheel. She pulled off her pirate hat and hung it on one of the spokes. Then she took Loretta's hand. She was ready to leave.

As Loretta led her to the door, Spark gazed up at her dusa, this girl who was becoming her own person.

"If Molly wakes up, you'll be able to . . . do something?" Spark said.

Loretta looked at her and smiled.

Then she opened the door.

THIRTY-FIVE

Spark awakened as she had on so many mornings, with her fluffy head resting on Loretta's chest. For a few disorienting seconds, she wondered if somehow she had traveled back to those old days, when monsters were merely a rumor. But one by one, she sensed all the things that did not belong. The harsh glare of the streetlamp overhead. A breeze that was far too strong for the inside of a bedroom. The groaning noise, like a tickle deep inside her ear that she could not scratch.

As Spark regained her balance, she realized that she was not lying in a bed but rather sitting upright on Loretta's lap. She pulled on the girl's collar. Loretta's head tipped forward. Her eyelids fluttered.

"Get back!" Reggie shouted. A mangler tried to test the bear's defenses by pawing at him. The creature wanted Mason's scratcher, which now hung from Reggie's belt. To keep it at bay, Reggie slashed his sword. It was a clumsy movement, but the monster withdrew its claw and continued pacing, probing for a weakness among the juro.

This standoff could not last much longer. With Jak overwhelmed, more manglers arrived to encircle the juro. Their instinctual fear of teddy bears kept them from attacking all at once. But their numbers grew. With or without orders from their master, they would soon

surge forward and it would all be over.

"Wake up!" Spark cried.

Loretta lifted her head but could not hold it steady.

"Can you hear me?" Spark said.

Loretta's eyes opened, but barely. When she saw Spark, she smiled as if she were about to tell a joke.

Loretta turned her attention to the brawl near the portal, where Jak looked to be expending the last of his strength fending off the manglers. His tail occasionally broke free from their grip, but more monsters came raining down from the cloud above.

Weakly, Loretta lifted her hand and pointed her palm toward the battle. Her arm stiffened. Her muscles locked and her tendons stretched taut as metal wires. It was exactly how she had looked when she opened the portal to pull Spark out of Jakmal's castle.

Meanwhile, the manglers stepped aside to let Karacor through. As he strode past, he peeked inside the small portal from which Jak and Mal had arrived. The smiling man shook his head. What a silly distraction this must have seemed to him. Bringing the monsters here merely delayed his inevitable victory.

While Spark clutched Loretta's shirt, Ozzie, Rana, and Lulu held their ground. They had retreated all the way to the chain-link fence, with nowhere left to go.

Karacor was savoring this moment. After all these years, the obstacles to his grand scheme had been whittled down to a trio of chubby bears and a doll masquerading as a warrior. He turned his attention to Loretta, the final key to his plan.

The manglers swarming Jak let out a great whooping sound as they toppled him over at last.

Where are you, Zed? Spark thought desperately.

Spark slid off Loretta's lap and squeezed between Ozzie and Lulu. As the leader of this juro, and she would stand beside them a

the end. Karacor would see what honor looked like.

"I'm sorry, everyone," Spark said.

"Don't be," Ozzie said. "I would rather be here than anywhere else in the world."

"I told you I'm not running away again," Rana said.

"Yeah, zip it, Spark," Lulu said. "We were all sitting in boxes before you gave us this adventure."

Spark waited for Reggie to say something. She wanted to hear one of Sir Reginald's old chestnuts. Something about how it didn't matter where they came from or where they were going—only what they did right now, in this moment. But with the tip of his sword still pointed at the enemy, daring them to come closer, the little black bear didn't need to say a word.

The rest of the manglers left Jakmal lying on the asphalt and turned their attention to the juro. A few of them glanced at Karacor, awaiting orders. He held out his hand, and the manglers grew still. He gave the bears one last smile and then snapped his fingers.

But before they had a chance to surge, another mangler flew through the air and collided with them. The ones in the front row toppled over like bowling pins.

Their guttural victory chant changed pitch. Something had sent them into a panic. Another mangler was flung from the rest. Its body smacked against the hospital wall and slid to the ground.

With the creatures growing more frenzied around her, Spark caught a glimpse of Karacor, the smile draining from his face. He lowered his arm as he saw his doom approaching.

The earth shook as two massive forms rose above the monsters. A pair of humans—knights wearing golden armor—swung their enormous broadswords. Though the visors on their helmets shielded their faces, Spark knew it was Jak and Mal, in their true forms, just as Sir Reginald had described them.

Spark turned to Loretta, the girl who had broken the curse. She was leaning back in her wheelchair, still dazed, probably thinking this was all a dream.

Jak and Mal cut their way through the army of manglers. A few tried to fight, only to get mowed down by the brothers' blades. One lunged for Jak's throat. The knight raised his gauntlet and smashed the creature, then hit it again with the hilt of his sword, knocking it out cold.

"There's Zed!" Lulu screamed in Spark's ear.

The monkey was crawling out of the smaller portal tail-first, dragging a large metal contraption with him. He looked so exhausted that he hardly noticed the panicked monsters racing about.

Spark pointed to Ozzie, Rana, and Lulu. "Get Loretta to the other side of the building. Understand?"

"You got it," Lulu said.

"Reggie, you're with me!" she shouted.

Spark and Reggie ran along the fence while the manglers tried to regroup. Their effort was fruitless. The rapidly expanding portal was dumping monsters everywhere—and not all of them bowed to Karacor. A massive lizard fought with something that resembled an octopus. A spider the size of a truck crawled toward Karacor as he tried to flee. A pack of manglers raced to protect him, biting the spider's legs to slow it down. Amid the chaos, Jak and Mal fought their way to Zed, shielding him as he struggled out of the portal.

The scratcher landed on the ground with a thud. Spark knelt by the side panel, locating the knobs that controlled the machine.

"How scary was it, Zed?" she asked.

The monkey gazed at the portal as it spiraled in the sky. "It was better than this!" he said. "At least I didn't—*oh my gosh look out!*"

Spark lifted her gaze in time to spot an open-mouthed mangler straight ahead. As it leapt toward them, a golden boot swung into its path and pinned it to the ground. Jak and Mal were providing cover for as long as they could.

"Gimme the little scratcher," Spark said. Reggie handed her Mason's device. "It needs to be on the highest setting."

"It already is!" Reggie said.

Just then, a giant squid plopped on the ground like a massive pile of spaghetti, smothering a group of manglers.

Spark tried to remember how to operate Jak's scratcher. She spun the dials all the way to the right, and the crystal at the end of the tube began to glow. On the display, the digital numbers fluctuated. And next to that, a shiny red button waited for her to press it. Spark wedged Mason's device between the knobs. Now both machines hummed and vibrated in unison.

Just then, Jak appeared beside her, his sword raised. The manglers formed a circle around him, hissing and snapping. Jak had lost his helmet, and his once-bald head flowed with golden hair, the same color as his armor.

Brushing the locks from his sweaty face, the knight spoke to Spark in the most sonorous voice she had ever heard, as if his throat were an organ in a cavernous church. "You have a plan." Not a question. A demand.

"Yeah!" Spark said. "Use both scratchers at the same time. Create a big portal. Big enough to swallow this one up."

The cloud still hovered over the hospital roof, nearly three stories high. "We must get the machine closer," Jak said.

"How do we do that?" Spark asked.

A mangler tried to take a bite out of Jak, but he jabbed it with the pommel of his sword. "Climb on board," he said. "The machine will remain in this world, so you just have to hold on. Whatever happens, do *not* let go."

Spark got on first, holding tight to the metal tube. Reggie hopped on behind her. He grabbed Zed by the arm and pulled him aboard.

"What does he mean, 'Do not let go'?" Zed asked.

Jak dropped his sword and gripped both sides of the scratcher. "On my mark," he said.

Spark placed her paw over the red button. She took one last look at Jak.

"Thank you," the knight said.

He heaved the scratcher into the air. The momentum pitched Spark's head back. Reggie held on to her, and Zed held on to him. They rose high above the battle, toward the swirling funnel cloud. At the exact weightless moment before they began to fall, Spark slammed her paw on the red button.

And strangely the weightless feeling remained. Zed's long tail floated in front of Spark's face. She batted it away and glanced over the side. They were suspended in the air, spinning slowly. Spark hugged the tube while Sir Reginald squeezed tighter around her waist.

Zed gasped. "Okay, we're floating. We're floating? We're *floating*!"

The crystal changed from white to bright blue, like the surface of Neptune. An azure-tinted aura extended from the machine, creating an enormous shimmering bubble that encompassed the swirling cloud overhead. This was no ordinary portal. The two scratchers, combined and ratcheted to their highest settings, had created a whirlpool that was sucking in the cloud. And at the same time . . .

"Spark, look!" Reggie shouted.

The monsters were lifting off the ground as the bubble engulfed them. They thrashed and kicked, trying to fight the invisible force, but it was no use. The enormous spider flailed its eight legs until it collided with the squid and became enmeshed in its tentacles. Soon, all the monsters were orbiting the scratcher while the blue bubble spun clockwise. The force of it dragged the cloud inside, scattering the vapor until it felt like they were flying inside a tornado.

Amid the floating bodies, a man in a black suit caught Spark's eye. Karacor grabbed one of the manglers and pushed himself away from it, launching his body toward the machine. His eyes were wide, and a white vein inflated on his head. His lips parted to reveal a row of gritted fangs. All of his calm and confidence were gone, replaced by rage at these meddlers who would dare keep him from his destiny.

He reached out his hand and caught Zed by the tail.

"Get off!" the monkey yelled. Reggie tried to hold him in place, but Zed's hands slid down the scratcher.

Reggie leapt from the machine. Spark felt his weight falling away. The black bear somersaulted past Zed and landed on Karacor's arm. With both paws, Reggie jabbed the tip of his sword into the man's sleeve. Karacor lost his grip. At the last possible second, Zed whipped his tail toward Reggie, who grabbed the very tip with his free paw.

Karacor grasped for them again, but it was too late. He plummeted into a swarming mass of manglers. He would get his wish to go home, but without the scratcher, and without Loretta.

They spun ever faster as the giant blue bubble began to collapse around them, with the crystal as the focal point. All the monsters were trapped inside. But Spark and her friends were safe as long as they did not let go. The monsters frantically tried to escape as the bubble shrank around them. The thunderous noise of the vortex drowned out their snarls. The bluish color glowed so bright that Spark shielded her eyes. And then came a brilliant flash of white and a sound as loud as a thunderclap.

The scratcher suddenly stopped spinning and plummeted to earth. Spark let go and bounced several times before rolling to a stop. The machine struck the ground and shattered into thousands of pieces.

Spark sat up. The cloud was gone. The wind had stopped. The monsters had vanished.

Zed lay on his back beside her. He rolled over and curled into a ball. "I would like to go back to my shelf now, please."

Reggie got to his feet and holstered his sword. A smoking bit of the machine had landed nearby, and he kicked it away.

He said exactly what Sir Reginald would have said at a time like this.

"Nice job, Hotshot. Nice job."

THIRTY-SIX

Not a trace of the storm remained. The wind from the vortex had blown away the clouds, revealing the stars in the sky.

Spark walked around the parking lot as she surveyed the damage. The spinning bubble that they created had swallowed a section of the fence, making it look like a giant had taken a bite out of it. Spark hoped that the humans would explain this away as a prank, the work of a couple of bored teenagers with bolt cutters. The damage to the hospital, however, would require a little more imagination. The vortex had sheared off the top corner of the building, a clean cut that almost looked like it was planned by the architect. In the morning, the person who worked in that office would be surprised to find they now had a skylight!

The two scratchers had been reduced to bits. The last of their kind, now smashed so completely that Spark could not tell which pieces went with which machine.

She was so distracted by the debris that she nearly forgot the most important thing. "Loretta!" she shouted.

Spark ran toward the other side of the hospital, with Reggie and Zed following close behind. She found Rana, Ozzie, and Lulu peeking around the corner.

Ozzie saw them coming and put a paw to his snout. "Shhhh."

They made room for Spark. The first thing she saw was the wheelchair, now empty. Loretta stood at the emergency door, her face bathed in the red glow of the exit sign. Confused and a little wobbly, she opened the door and went inside.

Spark made a move to follow her. The other bears grabbed her arms and held her in place.

"Can't go that way," Ozzie said. "It leads to the reception area. Too many humans. And they must be awake now."

The juro went back to the loading dock, in the rear of the building. On the way, Lulu plucked a piece of metal from the ground and examined it. "Whaddaya think? The humans will say the storm did all this damage?"

"They'll come up with something," Ozzie said.

Spark told them to split up again. "I want you all to head to the playroom. See who's still left from the Grand Sleuth."

"Where are *you* going?" Lulu asked.

"To visit an old friend."

As Spark was about to go inside, something shiny caught her eye. She stopped and gazed at the roof, where the two knights were watching from the ledge. Jak put on his helmet and folded his arms. Mal loomed behind him, slightly taller and wider. From where she stood, they resembled two massive statues, heroically set against the night sky.

The other juro members saw the brothers and stopped in their tracks. Zed was the last to notice. When he finally spotted them, his jaw dropped.

"Is your friend safe?" Jak asked.

"Yes, thank you," Spark said.

Jak whispered something to his brother.

"What about you?" Spark said. "Where will you go?"

219

"Mal thinks we should stay here for a while. To keep an eye on things. There are lots of children who could use a friend. A protector."

Spark held in a laugh. "Mal said all that?"

"He is quite persuasive," Jak said.

Spark supposed that the brothers wanted to make up for some of the bad things they had done. This seemed like the best place to start. There were children here who needed them, much like the boy they once protected.

"Stay brave, little bear," Jak said.

"Thanks," Spark said. "Good luck."

Spark headed inside, with the others following close behind.

Zed was slow to follow them. "Hey, how'd you guys get up there, anyway?" he said.

Lulu grabbed his hand and pulled him along.

THIRTY-SEVEN

As the juro entered the hospital, a piercing siren rang out. Someone had tripped the fire alarm, perhaps because they didn't know what else to do after waking from their trance. Somewhere on the highway, a fire engine approached, trumpeting its horn. There would be confusion for a while as the humans tried to figure out what had happened. In the end, they would concoct a rational explanation. A storm, an earthquake—anything that didn't include monsters, portals, or teddy bears. Sir Reginald used to say: "If you hear hoofbeats, think horses, not unicorns." In other words, the simplest explanation was almost always right. Almost.

The juro parted ways in the hall. Spark kept watch while the others ran to the playroom. At the end of the corridor, the murmuring from the reception area began to build. Over and over, Spark heard the same questions: "What was that? What just happened?" Someone asked why the automatic doors were broken. Another person was shouting about the ambulance crashed in the parking lot.

Spark hurried down the hall to Molly's room, where she found the door slightly open, wide enough for an old pink bear to slip through. She entered. The overhead lights were off. A desk lamp glowed on the nightstand.

Near the foot of the bed, Agnes sat on a chair. She held one arm over her chest to conceal a tear in her fur that ran from her neck to her leg. It was a clean cut, almost certainly from a mangler's claw.

"It's over, Agnes," Spark said.

The pink bear did not move.

"Can you hear me?"

Molly stirred in her bed. Acting on instinct, Spark dove under the chair.

Footsteps sounded from the hallway, approaching fast. "Molly!" someone yelled. Loretta appeared in the doorway, out of breath.

The fire alarm suddenly stopped as Molly sat up, rubbing her eyes. "What's happening?" she asked.

"I . . . don't know," Loretta said. "But everything's gonna be okay."

Matthew arrived. Judging from the look on his face, he was stunned to see his sister walking around. A few seconds later, Sofia appeared behind him. She took a step back when she saw Loretta.

"Are you all right?" Matthew said.

"I'm fine!" Loretta said. "I'm just checking on my friend." She turned to the little girl and said, "Molly, you know Matthew. And this is our friend Sofia."

"Hi," Molly said, trembling.

"Aw, it's okay!" Sofia said. "It was a scary storm, but it's over now."

Molly nodded but did not seem convinced.

"Hey, is that my *Jason and the Argonauts* poster?" Matthew said, pointing to the wall.

"You weren't using it," Loretta said.

Matthew rolled his eyes. He turned to Molly. "You know, I used to stay at this hospital too," he said.

"I know," Molly said.

"I'll tell you a secret." He leaned in and whispered: "There's a vending machine on the third floor that only doctors are supposed to use. Did you know that?"

"No."

"They made me promise not to tell anyone about it. It's got Oreos. And Kit Kats. Anything you want. You wanna sneak up there and get some? Everybody's runnin' around, so no one will notice."

"Matthew," Sofia said.

"I'm tryna help!"

"She is a pirate, after all," Loretta teased. "Let's go get some candy. Then we'll call your mom, okay?"

"Okay," the little girl said.

Molly reached for Loretta's hand. She took a few steps and then stopped in front of Agnes. Though the pink bear remained still, Spark could sense her regret, her desperation. She and Molly had been on so many adventures together. They had spent so many quiet nights here. Agnes hoped she could still make up for what she had done. While there was still time.

But the girl turned away and headed for the door. She had been through so much, and now she had new friends, new protectors. She no longer needed her teddy bear.

As Molly and the other children left, Agnes broke the rules and stretched out her arm. The tear in her fur grew wider as she reached for her dusa, begging her to return. But it was too late. Molly was gone. Agnes lowered her paw and slumped in her seat.

Spark climbed onto the chair and stood beside her. The old bear seemed locked into place.

"Everything I did was for her," Agnes said. "All of it."

"I know," Spark said.

"This is what it looks like," Agnes said. "The final light can take you away in the middle of a thought you're thinking. In the middle of a sentence you're speaking. The world won't even give you a chance to say goodbye."

"You said we were extensions of the children," Spark said. "So do we really die? Maybe we become a part of them."

Agnes snorted. "Either way, we're all alone."

Spark held out her paw. "You're not alone."

With great effort, Agnes took Spark's paw. The movement tore the last threads holding her fur together, widening the hole in her chest. Spark pretended not to notice.

"Karacor is gone," Spark said. "The children are safe."

"There will be other monsters," Agnes replied.

"And there will be other bears."

"You foolish young cub," Agnes said, barely able to move her mouth. "That was our last chance for peace. And now you think you can win an unwinnable war."

"Who said anything about winning?"

Agnes tried to turn her head.

"We'll keep fighting even if we don't know we'll win," Spark said. "Even if we *can't* win. Because it's the right thing to do. It's who we are. Who we've chosen to be."

The proud old bear wasn't used to someone lecturing her. "So be it. It's your fight now, Spark."

Agnes looked at the empty bed where Molly had left the covers barely hanging on the mattress.

"Were you ever able to connect with Loretta?" she asked. "The way I showed you?"

"Yes. Thank you."

"What did you learn?"

Spark thought about it. "That we can't stop the children from growing up," she said. "We can only help them along and hope for the best."

Agnes let out a wheezing laugh. "Hope," she said wistfully, as if recalling some faraway place.

Spark squeezed her paw. All she could do was be with Agnes at the end, to show her what hope could look like. They sat and listened to the voices in the halls, the sirens coming and going outside, the muffled announcements over the loudspeaker. Until finally Spark tugged on Agnes's paw and found it stiff and lifeless. The pink bear had become just another object in the room. The final light had arrived.

Spark needed to know one last truth. She gripped both sides of the hole in Agnes's chest and pulled the fabric apart, releasing a musty odor. Inside, Spark found a layer of dusty burlap. As she opened the hole further, the burlap took on a shape. It had stubby arms, a neck, and a face with a snout. This bear inside, Agnes's true form, had a single button for an eye to go along with its one ear. The first official teddy bears were invented in the early twentieth century, but this hunk of fabric was far older than that. Spark imagined this bear passing from one dusa to another, in orphanages and schools, boarding houses and hospitals, becoming worn and weathered almost beyond recognition.

"You've fulfilled your duty," Spark said. "Be at peace."

She pulled the hole together to conceal the ancient bear within. She left Agnes in her chair, perhaps for another child to discover someday.

THIRTY-EIGHT

Spark crept toward the doorway and poked her head out. Down the hall, Mr. Lopez stood with Sofia. He must have stopped her as she headed for the vending machine. The poor guy was just as confused as everyone else. From his perspective, his daughter had vanished right in front of him. Leaning forward with his hands on his hips, he kept asking her again and again if she was all right.

"I'm fine, Dad," she said. "We were looking for Loretta."

"And what happened to her? She was passed out one minute, then—"

"She's fine, too."

Mr. Lopez sighed while pinching the bridge of his nose.

"Dad, they're my friends. You always tell me the most important thing is to help people. And we were helping that little girl. She was scared."

Mr. Lopez said nothing. He knew his daughter was right.

"So let's go!" Sofia said. "That vending machine's on the third floor." She started to walk ahead while holding out her hand. "It has Kit Kats. Your favorite!"

Mr. Lopez sighed again. But then he grabbed her hand and followed his daughter.

Spark remained hidden while a team of nurses rolled a stretcher through the hallway. Once they passed, she made her way to the playroom. Pushing open the door, she saw all the bears of the Grand Sleuth huddled in a corner. Ozzie, Lulu, Zed, and Rana paced among them, keeping them in place. A few of the bears had clearly never seen an Amazon Princess™ before, complete with a crown and a pair of boots that clicked on the linoleum. They stared at her in awe.

Reggie, sword in hand, gestured toward the bears, as if to present Spark with a gift.

"They surrendered!" he said.

"I see that," she replied.

In the first row, Mason sat beside Iggy, who held his Christmas hat in his paws. A tire mark streaked across his flattened foot, a souvenir from the ambulance.

Spark approached Mason first. "You were expecting Agnes to come through that door?"

Mason would not look at her. "I told her you were dangerous," he said. "She would not listen. So go ahead. Do what you must."

"What *must* I do with you?"

Mason forced himself to face her. "Do not toy with me. You want revenge for what we did. So take it."

Spark crouched before him so they could see eye to eye. "You think, after all we went through, that I would start acting like *you*?"

At last, shame crept onto Mason's smug face.

"You still have a dusa," Spark said. "What's his name? Damon?"

Mason nodded.

"He's good at karate. And he likes ice cream. What flavor was it?"

"Chocolate-chip cookie dough."

"Chocolate-chip cookie dough," she repeated. "And Iggy. Your

227

dusa is Leah, right?"

"Yes," Iggy said.

"And where's that yellow bear?"

A yellow bear raised his paw.

"What's your dusa's name again?" Spark said.

"Natalie."

"Natalie, right."

She gave all of them a moment to remember the children they protected.

"You are all someone's teddy bear. You will act like it from here on out. If you don't, we'll be back."

At this, Iggy nervously crushed his hat into a tight red ball.

"I'm dismissing your high council," Spark said. "From now on, you'll be good little bears, watching over your children. Because we'll be watching *you*."

"There *must* be a Grand Sleuth!" Mason cried. "You cannot dismantle the high council!"

"You dismantled it yourself. By helping the enemy."

"Please," Mason said. "It is true, we failed. But there has always been a Grand Sleuth."

Spark glanced at her friends. All of them—even Zed—seemed to have the same idea.

"In that case," Spark said, "you're looking at the new Grand Sleuth."

Mason's face dropped.

"Happy now?" Lulu said.

"We're gonna start spreading the word," Spark said. "Now, you have your orders. So get back in your toy box!"

Grateful to be spared, the bears ran to the box and stuffed themselves inside. Mason was the last to join them. He he jumped into the box and glared at Spark as he lowered the lid.

The juro gathered in the center of the floor.

"You have answered the call," Spark said to her friends. "I can't begin to tell you how grateful I am."

"You led us well," Ozzie said. The others nodded in agreement.

"Are we really gonna be the Grand Sleuth?" Zed asked.

"We'll lead by example," Spark said.

She motioned for Reggie to step forward. "The last time we fought together, I was supposed to release everyone from their oath," Spark said. "But I couldn't recall the words. You're the only one who might remember them."

Reggie rested his hands on his belt. "If I say the words, then the juro is over?"

Before she answered, Spark looked them all square in the eye. Ozzie the strong polar bear. Lulu the clever panda. Zed, the sock monkey who found his courage. Rana, the Amazon who lived up to her name. And finally, Reggie, once the great bear who had trained her, now on his way to becoming a great bear once again.

"Yes," Spark said. "The juro will end."

Reggie nodded. "In that case, I don't remember the words."

Spark could have hugged him in that moment, but she held it together.

"We have a long march ahead of us," she said. "Let's practice telling our stories."

For the rest of the night, through the parks and the backyards, through the streets and the alleys, they each took a turn reciting their version of the adventure until what was exaggerated blended with what was true. A new legend for the League of Ursus.

THIRTY-NINE

Despite all the chaos at the hospital, the unexplained power out-ages, and the damage from the storm, the film festival commenced that weekend on schedule. People streamed into the gymnasium to see the exhibits. The organizers piped in the soundtracks of famous movies. Spark recognized the music from *Raiders of the Lost Ark*, *Back to the Future*, *Rocky*, *Frozen*, and *Moana*. In the evening, the adjacent theater would play the movies in the competition.

For Spark, behaving like a normal teddy bear, without all the sneaking around and hopping through portals, came as a welcome relief. All she needed to do was stay in the display case as people ambled by, holding their event brochures. Onlookers stopped and stared at the poster, which showed the stuffed animals ready for their swashbuckling adventure. Then their heads would swivel to the case as they realized that these were in fact the stars of the movie. Children pressed their faces against the glass to get a good look at the toys inside.

Spark eavesdropped on conversations, hoping to hear what peo-ple were saying about the events of the day before. Most thought it was just a really bad, highly localized storm. One man insisted it was the hospital pulling an insurance scam. Later, a woman on her cellphone talked to her mom about the ambulance that was stolen from the hospital parking lot and taken for a joyride. They were still looking for the culprit.

Spark found this all so amusing that she didn't even notice Sofia peering into the display case until the girl's nose bumped the glass. With her hair twisted into two braids and a huge smile on her face, no one would know that she had recently been placed under a spell while the sky split open and monsters fell out.

"Here it is!" she said.

Mr. Lopez appeared behind her, wearing his uniform. He had left work early to attend.

"These are the stars of the movie," Sofia said.

"What, did they make them dance around or something?" Mr. Lopez said. "Like puppets?"

"Pretty much."

"Hey, why didn't you use *your* bear for the movie?" he said.

"He got lost when we moved into the apartment."

Mr. Lopez lowered his head. Mentioning the move must have brought back bad memories for them both.

To Spark's relief, she heard Loretta's voice in the crowd. "Hey, Sofia!"

Loretta and Matthew each gave Sofia a hug, right before awkwardly saying hello to Mr. Lopez. Sofia asked Loretta how she was feeling.

"They ran a bunch of tests on me until, like, two in the morning," Loretta said. "But I'm fine. They just told me to get some sleep."

"Wow, look at all this," Matthew said, marveling at the booth. Next to the poster, someone had hung his movie storyboards on the walls.

"They're doing temporary tattoos in a booth over there," Loretta said to Sofia. She rolled up the sleeve of her hoodie. "Look."

On her forearm, painted with black ink, were two symbols: a projector aimed at the face of a bear. The symbols reminded Spark of the hieroglyphs that the League used to communicate.

Matthew tugged at his sleeve to reveal his own. "Might be our new logo," he said. "I'm not sure yet."

Mr. Lopez leaned over them. "What is that? Is that, like, a symbol for a club? Or a gang?"

"Sort of," Matthew said.

"Yeah, it's *our* gang," Loretta said. "We've been solving some mysteries lately."

Mr. Lopez squinted at her. "Mysteries."

"Mysteries about life, Dad," Sofia said.

While Mr. Lopez nodded and pursed his lips, the children exchanged knowing glances. Spark could only guess what they really knew, or what Loretta could recall from the night before. It was enough for them to have this inside joke, a secret world they were just beginning to discover, and that the grown-ups could never fully understand.

"You have tickets to the movie, right?" Matthew said.

Sofia pulled them from her pocket.

"Oh, you're two rows behind us," he said.

Loretta reminded Matthew that they needed to find their parents and bring them over to the exhibit. The children said their goodbyes, for now. As Matthew passed Sofia, she glanced at her father to make sure he wasn't looking. And then, barely containing a giggle, she reached out and squeezed his hand. Spark expected him to be surprised, but Matthew squeezed back and smiled. They both let go as soon as Mr. Lopez turned around.

Mr. Lopez gave the siblings a polite smile as they left. As soon as they were out of earshot, he blurted out, "That boy has a crush on you."

Lulu snorted. "Yeah, ya think?" she whispered.

Sofia covered her face with her hands. "Oh my gosh, Dad, shut up!"

Mr. Lopez allowed himself a chuckle before changing the subject. "This is, uh . . . this is cool stuff you're doing. This movie stuff."

"Thanks," Sofia said.

"With some good people," he added.

"Yeah."

Mr. Lopez nodded. "All right, you wanna get this weird tattoo? So you can be in a gang with your friends?"

As they walked away, Sofia said, "It's not actually a gang, Dad."

Once they were gone, the bears could finally chat.

"That's it?" Lulu said. "He shoulda said, 'I'm sorry, I was wrong about your friends.' Or 'I love you.'"

"That would have been nice," Ozzie said.

"It's a start," Spark said.

She remembered Agnes at the final light. It was too late for her to fix things. It wasn't too late for these two.

"A start's better than nothing," Ozzie said.

"Especially if it's a new start!" Rana said.

Spark liked the sound of that. A new start. That's what they had, too. As the new Grand Sleuth, they were charting their own course. The thought made Spark excited and terrified at the same time. And then she realized that this must be what growing up felt like.

If Loretta could do it, then so could she.

FORTY

The exhibit hall closed at five. The lights dimmed. Though Spark found the display case stuffy, at least her friends were with her.

In the theater, people took their seats. Spark could hear someone speaking on a microphone—probably the host welcoming everyone and introducing the competition. She remembered the time that she and Sir Reginald had accompanied the family to a viewing of *Clash of the Titans*, when Loretta was still a baby who needed her teddy bear to feel safe. Spark imagined the family now, seated in a row, the screen lighting up their faces.

"Hey, Spark," Ozzie said, "we've decided to give you a little present." Lulu, Rana, and Zed leaned closer to see her reaction.

Spark looked around. She didn't see anything inside the case that they could give her.

"That's nice of you. What is it?"

Lulu pulled her lock-picking tools from her fur and opened the case.

Despite all the risks they had taken in the last few days, Spark was still nervous. "Hey, we've already pushed our luck too far as it is."

"Don't worry, you're gonna like this," Lulu said, right before dropping to the floor and scurrying away.

"What could I possibly need?" Spark said. "Zed, are *you* okay with this?"

"Of course not! But I'm doing it anyway. Just like you taught me."

"This is mutiny!"

"But it's a *nice* mutiny," Ozzie said.

A few seconds later, a small table on wheels rolled toward them and parked beside the case. A black tablecloth covered the top. From underneath, Lulu parted the cloth and stuck her head out.

"Your limo has arrived," Rana said. "We're going to the red carpet!"

"First sign of trouble, and we come back, okay?" Spark said. Though, really, this *was* the first sign of trouble.

They all jumped out of the display case and joined Lulu under the cloth. Each one took a position at a wheel, pushing the cart forward. Zed straddled the metal bar that connected the axles and helped steer. The contraption moved toward the wall, then made a left, heading for the side entrance to the theater. The metal door opened quietly, leading to a small alcove under the balcony.

The first film in the competition was playing on the screen. It was *Tender Hearts*, a romantic story in which a young man makes googly eyes at a woman in a coffee shop. The actors' voices boomed through the speakers.

Spark spotted her family in one of the last rows. Matthew was whispering something to Loretta. A few times, he stole a glance at the last row, where Sofia sat with her father.

When the screen brightened again, Spark saw Molly seated directly in front of Loretta. While her mom seemed puzzled by the film, Molly watched with her hands folded under her chin, the image reflected in her eyes like two little movie screens. This may have been her first trip to the cinema in a long time. She was enjoying every moment.

Nearby, something shiny in the crowd caught the light. It was Claire, dressed in a sequined evening gown as if she were attending the Academy Awards, just as she had promised. She wore a fancy hairdo, her bun piled so high that the man behind her had to lean to the side to see the screen. Spark turned to Rana, her eyebrows raised.

"It's a big night for her!" Rana whispered.

"She should wear a crown like you!" Lulu said.

Next to her were Jisha and Darcy, wearing plain sweaters and jeans. Spark imagined Claire begging her friends to go formal and the two of them rolling their eyes at her.

Just as Spark was wishing Reggie could be there to see this, she spotted Jared with his mother. A backpack rested on his lap, unzipped, and a familiar pair of fuzzy black ears poked out. The bear must have sensed the juro nearby, for his ears turned toward them—and then he looked right at Spark and winked. The old Sir Reginald never would have broken the rules like that. But Reggie was a different bear. A little plastic face popped up beside him. It was Officer Hogan, tagging along for the adventure. Jared didn't even notice; his eyes were fixed on the screen.

The romantic movie ended, and more short films followed. Safely hidden, the juro watched a documentary on a local bodega, a parody of *Star Wars* in which all the characters were played by dogs, a cartoon about a time-traveling robot and his pet iguana, a black-and-white detective movie, and a music video by a local hip-hop group that made everyone's heads bob in unison.

Finally, the screen went dark. The logo for Matthew and Loretta's YouTube channel appeared: AN LM^2 PRODUCTION. The audience went wild—some of them probably remembered the kids' film from last year's contest. Everyone fell silent when the title replaced the logo. A jaunty musical score began, and the screen faded to an image of a roaring fire. In the foreground, paper cutouts of warriors advanced from either side, creating silhouettes against the flames. They clashed in the middle amid the sounds of grunting and swords clanging. It was beautiful—like someone telling a story at a campfire.

"The great war tore our kingdom asunder," Loretta's voiceover said. "Our king was lost. The entire country burned. But then a handful of heroes banded together to find the king, rescue him, and restore him to the throne . . ."

With that, the movie cut to a shot of Spark, Zed, Rana, and Lulu facing the camera. After such a melodramatic prologue, the sight of stuffed animals trying to look tough made the audience hysterical with laughter. A group of college students in the front row laughed the hardest, with a few pumping their fists as though their favorite sports team had won a championship.

The story zipped along from there, with Spark's character leading the charge through swamps and dungeons, dense forests and barren mountains—all re-created with household items in Loretta's living room. Spark remembered filming every shot. When she swung on a rope from the stairs to the sofa, the audience cheered. When Zed clung to the edge of a cliff, everyone held their breath. When Lulu came face-to-face with a dragon, they rooted for her to fight.

Eventually, Spark stopped watching the screen and focused on the audience and their reactions. Loretta, Matthew, and Sofia had created a window into a new world, like a portal, and everyone in the room had fallen into it—especially Molly, who watched the entire movie with her hands on her cheeks and her mouth agape. It was a perfect moment shared with hundreds of people. Spark recalled what Agnes had said, how the final light could arrive at any moment. If it happened here, the last thing she would see would be the juro on this giant screen saving the day.

Which kind of made sense.

But she was still here, marveling at this strange and silly story that her dusa had crafted. Somehow, the young filmmakers had crammed this epic tale into a fifteen-minute movie, which ended with the good guys winning, of course. The audience, especially the college students in front, seemed willing to overlook the plot holes. As the credits rolled, a few people stood and clapped.

Loretta gave a thumbs-up to Jisha, Claire, and Darcy. Matthew couldn't resist exchanging a glance with Sofia. She giggled and waved at him. Then she pulled her sleeve from her wrist to reveal the symbol tattooed on her forearm. Matthew pointed to his own. Mr. Lopez raised an eyebrow at them but said nothing.

The screen went dark again and another film started, but the audience was still clapping. The projectionist paused for a minute to let the crowd settle.

"Time to go," Ozzie said.

"I wanna see the awards ceremony," Spark said.

"Gotta get back before everyone leaves the theater," Lulu said.

"We're still in mutiny mode," Rana added. "We're not following your orders right now."

Spark couldn't argue. They were right. She helped them steer the table through the exit and across the exhibit floor toward the booth. Once they were sure no one was around, they ditched their "limo" and walked the rest of the way. Without a word, they climbed into the display case and shut the lid.

Spark could still hear the applause ringing in her ears. She had seen things that few bears would ever see. Rather than be sad that her adventure was over, she was filled with an overwhelming sense of gratitude, a weightless sensation that made her feel light enough to float.

"Thank you," she said to her friends.

But really, she was sending her thanks beyond this tiny space, out into the world. She would hold on to this feeling for as long as she could. And if she ever lost it, she would drop everything she was doing to find it again.

FORTY-ONE

From her usual spot on the shelf in Loretta's room, Spark could pretend, for a few minutes at a time, that nothing had changed. That Jak and Mal had never arrived, that Sir Reginald still watched over Matthew's room, that the Grand Sleuth was still in hiding. She could not say exactly why it felt good to do this. Perhaps because it reminded her of how far she had come.

Before she got too lost in nostalgia, she leaned forward and peered out the window. There, under the windowsill of Jared's room, Reggie had drawn a new set of symbols that would soon wash off in the rain. Even if a human recognized them as some kind of hieroglyphic language, they would never be able to decipher them. Starting from the left, the message showed a bear's head: a circle with two crescent shapes on top. Next to that were a crown, a sword, a lightning bolt. And at the end of the line, a trumpet.

Together, it meant that the Grand Sleuth was here, in this town. As Agnes would say, the Grand Sleuth went where it was needed. The trumpet was a call to all the bears out there to spread the word, and to step forward. No more would the leadership be limited to a few warriors trying to fend off the final light. Just as there would be new monsters, there would be new bears—and other toys!—to pass the torch. To keep the fire going. Spark had drawn the same message on her house. It would spread from there. The other warriors fighting the good fight would know that they were not alone.

For the entire afternoon, Spark sat on the shelf below Zed while Loretta tapped away on her computer. She was writing a new screenplay. A mystery, like she'd promised Mom and Dad a few days earlier. Spark read the opening lines on the bright white screen.

```
EXT. SUBURBAN STREET — DAY
We start with a tracking shot, moving along a
suburban street. We pass all the nice houses until
we arrive at the parking lot for an abandoned
hospital. The windows are boarded up. Stalks of
grass poke out of the cracked pavement. A sign
says "KEEP OUT." A creepy place.
```

Ah, the abandoned wing of the hospital. Maybe this movie was part mystery, part documentary. A way for her to make sense of everything that had happened.

Loretta typed the letters *V.O.* That meant voiceover—a narrator who introduces a scene. Beneath that, she wrote:

```
Do you believe in monsters?
```

"What are you writing?" Matthew asked from the doorway.

Loretta pulled the internet browser over the screenplay. "Can you knock first?"

"The door was open."

"That doesn't mean come in!"

Matthew entered anyway, wearing a brand-new Young Filmmakers Award T-shirt. This year's version was navy blue instead of gray. Spark had learned that their movie won the Spirit Award, the same category they had won the year before. A year ago, Matthew would have fumed over this outcome. He wanted the top prize so badly. But he was older now and knew that winning the award meant that they had created something special, something that brought a little joy into the world. Besides, they had more important things to think about.

"Are we heading out or what?" Loretta asked.

"Yeah, I'm ready! Why aren't you?"

It was Saturday, which meant they were going to the hospital. Someone had beaten Matthew in the video game contest the week before, and he vowed to reclaim his title. Loretta was planning to bring Spark for another visit to Molly's pirate ship. Molly insisted that her ship needed a new first mate, someone who had survived many adventures. Spark deserved a promotion from ship's cook.

"I'll be down in a minute," Loretta said.

Matthew eyed the computer screen.

"That means I'll meet you downstairs," Loretta said.

"Fine," he said. "But you're showin' me the new script later."

"I'm showin' you when I wanna show you!"

After Matthew left the room, Loretta paced while running her hands through her thick hair, a process that often took several tries until she bunched it into a bun at the top of her head. She grabbed her backpack and opened it. Then she turned to Spark and stopped, as if noticing her for the first time.

There was no way for Spark to know what Loretta remembered from their encounter in the dreamworld. Loretta may have dismissed it as a product of her imagination. But it was in her heart now. It was a part of her, a part of both of them. Whether they were saving the world or playing a game in the backyard, the adventure of discovery—the challenge to be brave and true—remained the same.

We can only help them along, and hope for the best.

Loretta took Spark from the shelf and was about to drop the bear into her backpack. But then she stopped and held Spark at arm's length, staring right into her eyes. As if she were trying to remember something. Or as if a memory had risen to the surface.

Framed in the light from the window, Loretta no longer seemed a child to Spark—she was a new person, someone the world would soon meet. There was more learning to do; that never ended. There would be mistakes. Fear. Regret. But here she was, every bit the warrior that Spark had become.

Spark was so proud of her dusa. She was so happy to have seen her this far.

She was—

ACKNOWLEDGMENTS

Wow, sequels are really hard to write! And I'm so grateful to the many people who helped to bring this book to you, despite the difficulties of the past year.

First, I owe so much to my agent Jennifer Weltz, who landed my weird series with an amazing publisher. At Quirk, my editor Rebecca Gyllenhaal took a chance on my first book, and then worked her magic to get a follow-up into shape within a year. I am in awe of the passion and dedication that she put into this, and I'm so proud to have worked with her. Thanks also go to the people at Quirk who supported this series, including Katherine McGuire, Kelsey Hoffman, Nicole de Jackmo, Brett Cohen, Christina Tatulli, Jhanteigh Kupihea, John J. McGurk, Elissa Flanigan, Jane Morley, and Mary Ellen Wilson. I'm also grateful to the artists for this series, Ryan Andrews and James Firnhaber, who perfectly captured the tone of the book in their designs.

A special thank you for my fellow writers who blurbed the first book in this series, including Natalie Lloyd, Tania del Rio, J.W. Ocker, J.A. White, and Kirsten Miller. Thanks also to my friends and colleagues at Oxford University Press and Gotham Writers' Workshop, especially Anna-Lise Santella and Kelly Caldwell, who have always been supportive of my work.

To my friends who have stayed in New York, and those who have been scattered, thank you for your encouragement, both in person and through a Zoom window. And finally, my deep and sincere thanks to Ashley Wells, for patience, listening, and inspiration.

About The Author

Nicholas Repino

ROBERT REPINO is the author of *Mort(e)*, *Culdesac*, and *D'Arc*, which make up the critically acclaimed War with No Name series (Soho Press). He holds an MFA in creative writing from Emerson College and teaches at the Gotham Writers' Workshop. By day, he's an editor at a scholarly press. The League of Ursus series is his middle-grade debut. He lives in New York City.

Growing up, Robert had two special teddy bears: Bear and Blue Bear.